'You are going to stay at that door all day and all night, and for many a long year,' said the Fairy Blackstick to the hall porter, and promptly turned him into a door-knocker.

That was at the time of the Princess Angelica's christening, and he was to stay there on the door another twenty years while some most amazing events took place. It was a confusing time for everyone except the Fairy Blackstick, what with two usurpations, the adventures of the rightful heirs, and a dreadful battle complicated by a magic sword of fantastic power.

Most remarkable of all was the way the four princes and princesses in the story fell in and out of love with each other, all because of the Fairy Blackstick's two magical presents: a rose and a ring.

William Thackeray was already a famous literary figure when he wrote and illustrated the story more than a hundred years ago. He called it 'a fireside pantomime', and that exactly describes its mixture of fairy tale and humour, of fantasy and slapstick.

William Makepeace Thackeray was born in Calcutta in 1811. At the age of six, he was sent to school in England. He went on to Cambridge University, but left after a few terms. In 1831 he started reading for the bar, but soon gave that up, and spent three years in Paris studying art. In 1836, he married and started work in earnest as a journalist.

He attracted attention as a satirist when he began writing for *Punch* in 1842. In 1847 his great novel *Vanity Fair* began to appear in monthly numbers, followed by *Pendennis*, *Esmond*, and *The Newcomes*. In 1853 he went to Rome with his two daughters and there wrote *The Rose and the Ring*. By the time Thackeray died in 1863, he had achieved permanent fame as a satirical novelist.

W. M. THACKERAY

THE ROSE AND THE RING

OR

The History of Prince Giglio and Prince Bulbo

—

A FIRESIDE PANTOMIME FOR GREAT AND SMALL CHILDREN

PUFFIN BOOKS

PUFFIN BOOKS

Published by the Penguin Group
27 Wrights Lane, London W8 5TZ, England
Viking Penguin Inc., 40 West 23rd Street, New York, New York 10010, USA
Penguin Books Australia Ltd, Ringwood, Victoria, Australia
Penguin Books Canada Ltd, 2801 John Street, Markham, Ontario, Canada L3R 1B4
Penguin Books (NZ) Ltd, 182–190 Wairau Road, Auckland 10, New Zealand

Penguin Books Ltd, Registered Offices: Harmondsworth, Middlesex, England

First published 1855
Published in Puffin Books 1964
Reprinted 1967, 1972, 1988

Set in Monotype Modern No. 7
Revisions set by Merrion Letters, London

Printed and bound in Great Britain by
Cox & Wyman Ltd, Reading

Prelude

IT happened that the undersigned spent the last Christmas season in a foreign city where there were many English children.

In that city, if you wanted to give a child's party, you could not even get a magic lantern or buy Twelfth-Night characters – those funny painted pictures of the King, the Queen, the Lover, the Lady, the Dandy, the Captain, and so on – with which our young ones are wont to recreate themselves at this festive time.

My friend, Miss Bunch, who was governess of a large family, that lived in the *Piano Nobile* of the house inhabited by myself and my young charges (it was the Palazzo Poniatowski at Rome, and Messrs. Spillmann, two of the best pastry-cooks in Christendom, have their shop on the ground-floor); Miss Bunch, I say, begged me to draw a set of Twelfth Night characters for the amusement of our young people.

She is a lady of great fancy and droll imagination, and having looked at the characters, she and I composed a history about them, which was recited to the little folks at night, and served as our FIRESIDE PANTOMIME.

Our juvenile audience was amused by the adventures of Giglio and Bulbo, Rosalba and Angelica. I am bound to say the fate of the Hall Porter created a considerable sensation; and the wrath of Countess Gruffanuff was received with extreme pleasure.

If these children are pleased, thought I, why should not others be amused also? In a few days Dr Birch's young friends will be expected to reassemble at Rodwell Regis, where they will learn everything that is useful, and under the eyes of careful ushers continue the business of their little lives.

But, in the meanwhile, and for a brief holiday, let us laugh and be as pleasant as we can. And you elder folks – a little joking, and dancing, and fooling will do even you no harm. The author wishes you a merry Christmas, and welcomes you to the Fireside Pantomime.

December, 1854   M. A. TITMARSH

1

Shows how the royal family sate down to breakfast

THIS is Valoroso XXIV, King of Paflagonia, seated with his Queen and only child at their royal breakfast-table, and receiving the letter which announces to his Majesty a proposed visit from Prince Bulbo, heir of Padella, reigning King of Crim Tartary. Remark the delight upon the monarch's royal features. He is so absorbed in the perusal of the King of Crim Tartary's letter, that he allows his eggs to get cold, and leaves his august muffins untasted.

'What! that wicked, brave, delightful Prince Bulbo!' cries Princess Angelica; 'so handsome, so accomplished, so witty – the conqueror of Rimbombamento, where he slew ten thousand giants!'

'Who told you of him, my dear?' asks his Majesty.

'A little bird,' says Angelica.

'Poor Giglio!' says mamma, pouring out the tea.

'Bother Giglio!' cries Angelica, tossing up her head, which rustled with a thousand curl-papers.

'I wish,' growls the King – 'I wish Giglio was . . .'

'Was better? Yes, dear, he is better,' says the Queen. 'Angelica's little maid, Betsinda, told me so when she came to my room this morning with my early tea.'

'You are always drinking tea,' said the Monarch, with a scowl.

'It is better than drinking port or brandy-and-water,' replies her Majesty.

'Well, well, my dear, I only said you were fond of drinking tea,' said the King of Paflagonia, with an effort as if to command his temper. 'Angelica! I hope you have plenty of new dresses; your milliners' bills are long enough. My dear Queen, you must see and have some parties. I prefer dinners, but of course you will be for balls. Your everlasting blue velvet quite tires me: and, my love, I should like you to have a new necklace. Order one. Not more than a hundred or a hundred and fifty thousand pounds.'

'And Giglio, dear,' says the Queen.

'GIGLIO MAY GO TO THE –'

'Oh, sir,' screams her Majesty. 'Your own nephew! our late King's only son.'

'Giglio may go to the tailor's, and order the bills to be sent in to Glumboso to pay. Confound him! I mean bless his dear heart. He need want for nothing; give him a couple of guineas for pocket-money, my dear; and you may as well order yourself bracelets, while you are about the necklace, Mrs V.'

Her Majesty, or *Mrs V.*, as the monarch facetiously called her (for even royalty will have its sport, and this august family were very much attached), embraced her husband, and, twining her arm round her daughter's waist, they quitted the breakfast-room in order to make all things ready for the princely stranger.

When they were gone, the smile that had lighted up the eyes of the *husband* and *father* fled – the pride of the *King* fled – the MAN was alone. Had I the pen of a G. P. R. James, I would describe Valoroso's torments in the choicest language; in which I would also depict his flashing eye, his distended nostril – his dressing-gown, pocket-handkerchief, and boots. But I need not say I have *not* the pen of that novelist; suffice it to say, Valoroso was alone.

He rushed to the cupboard, seizing from the table one of the many egg-cups with which his princely board was served for the matin meal, drew out a bottle of right Nantz or Cognac, filled and emptied the cup several times, and laid it down with a hoarse 'Ha, ha, ha! now Valoroso is a man again.

'But oh!' he went on (still sipping, I am sorry to say), 'ere I was a king, I needed not this intoxicating draught; once I detested the hot brandy wine, and quaffed no other fount but nature's rill. It dashes not more quickly o'er the rocks, than I did, as, with blunderbuss in hand, I brushed away the early morning dew, and shot the partridge, snipe, or antlered deer! Ah! well may England's dramatist remark, "Uneasy lies the head that wears a crown!" Why did I steal my nephew's, my young Giglio's –? Steal! said I? no, no, no, not steal, not steal. Let me withdraw that odious expression. I took, and on my manly head I set, the royal crown of Paflagonia; I took, and with my royal arm I wield,

9

the sceptral rod of Paflagonia; I took, and in my out-
stretched hand I hold, the royal orb of Paflagonia! Could a
poor boy, a snivelling, drivelling boy – was in his nurse's
arms but yesterday, and cried for sugar-plums and puled for
pap – bear up the awful weight of crown, orb, sceptre? gird
on the sword my royal fathers wore, and meet in fight the
tough Crimean foe?'

And then the monarch went on to argue in his own mind
(though we need not say that blank verse is not argument)
that what he had got it was his duty to keep, and that, if at
one time he had entertained ideas of a certain restitution,
which shall be nameless, the prospect by a *certain marriage*
of uniting two crowns and two nations which had been engaged in bloody and expensive wars, as the Paflagonians and
the Crimeans had been, put the idea of Giglio's restoration
to the throne out of the question: nay, were his own brother,
King Savio, alive, he would certainly will away the crown
from his own son in order to bring about such a desirable
union.

Thus easily do we deceive ourselves! Thus do we fancy
what we wish is right! The King took courage, read the
papers, finished his muffins and eggs, and rang the bell for
his Prime Minister. The Queen, after thinking whether she
should go up and see Giglio, who had been sick, thought
'Not now. Business first; pleasure afterwards. I will go and
see dear Giglio this afternoon; and now I will drive to the
jeweller's, to look for the necklace and bracelets.' The Princess went up into her own room, and made Betsinda, her
maid, bring out all her dresses; and as for Giglio, they forgot
him as much as I forget what I had for dinner last Tuesday
twelvemonth.

2

How King Valoroso got the crown, and Prince Giglio went without

PAFLAGONIA, ten or twenty thousand years ago, appears to have been one of those kingdoms where the laws of succession were not settled; for when King Savio died, leaving his brother Regent of the kingdom, and guardian of Savio's orphan infant, this unfaithful regent took no sort of regard of the late monarch's will; had himself proclaimed sovereign of Paflagonia under the title of King Valoroso XXIV, had a most splendid coronation, and ordered all the nobles of the kingdom to pay him homage. So long as Valoroso gave them plenty of balls at Court, plenty of money and lucrative places, the Paflagonian nobility did not care who was king; and, as for the people, in those early times they were equally indifferent. The Prince Giglio, by reason of his tender age at his royal father's death, did not feel the loss of his crown and empire. As long as he had plenty of toys and sweetmeats, a holiday five times a week, and a horse and gun to go out shooting when he grew a little older, and, above all, the company of his darling cousin, the King's only child, poor Giglio was perfectly contented; nor did he envy his uncle the royal robes and sceptre, the great hot uncomfortable throne of state, and the enormous cumbersome crown in which that monarch appeared from morning till night. King Valoroso's portrait has been left to us; and I think you will agree with me that he must have been sometimes *rather tired* of his velvet, and his diamonds, and his ermine, and his grandeur. I

11

shouldn't like to sit in that stifling robe, with such a thing as that on my head.

No doubt, the Queen must have been lovely in her youth; for though she grew rather stout in after life, yet her features, as shown in her portrait, are certainly *pleasing*. If she was

fond of flattery, scandal, cards, and fine clothes, let us deal gently with her infirmities, which, after all, may be no greater than our own. She was kind to her nephew; and if she had any scruples of conscience about her husband's taking the young Prince's crown, consoled herself by thinking that

the King, though a usurper, was a most respectable man, and that at his death Prince Giglio would be restored to his throne, and share it with his cousin, whom he loved so fondly.

The Prime Minister was Glumboso, an old statesman, who most cheerfully swore fidelity to King Valoroso, and in whose hands the monarch left all the affairs of his kingdom. All Valoroso wanted was plenty of money, plenty of hunting, plenty of flattery, and as little trouble as possible. As long as he had his sport, this monarch cared little how his people paid for it: he engaged in some wars, and of course the Paflagonian newspapers announced that he gained prodigious victories: he had statues erected to himself in every city of the empire; and of course his pictures placed everywhere, and in all the print-shops: he was Valoroso the Magnanimous, Valoroso the Victorious, Valoroso the Great, and so forth; – for even in these early early times courtiers and people knew how to flatter.

This royal pair had one only child, the Princess Angelica, who, you may be sure, was a paragon in the courtiers' eyes, in her parents', and in her own. It was said she had the longest hair, the largest eyes, the slimmest waist, the smallest foot, and the most lovely complexion of any young lady in the Paflagonian dominions. Her accomplishments were announced to be even superior to her beauty; and governesses used to shame their idle pupils by telling them what Princess Angelica could do. She could play the most difficult pieces of music at sight. She could answer any one of 'Mangnal's Questions'. She knew every date in the history of Paflagonia, and every other country. She knew French, English, Italian, German, Spanish, Hebrew, Greek, Latin, Cappadocian, Samothracian, Aegean, and Crim Tartar. In a word, she was a most accomplished young creature; and her governess and lady-in-waiting was the severe Countess Gruffanuff.

Would you not fancy, from this picture, that Gruffanuff must have been a person of the highest birth? She looks so haughty that I should have thought her a Princess at the very least, with a pedigree reaching as far back as the Deluge. But this lady was no better born than many other ladies who give themselves airs; and all sensible people laughed at her absurd pretensions. The fact is, she had been maid-servant to the Queen when her Majesty was only Princess, and her husband had been head footman; but after his death or *disappearance*,

of which you shall hear presently, this Mrs Gruffanuff, by flattering, toadying, and wheedling her royal mistress, became a favourite with the Queen (who was rather a weak woman), and her Majesty gave her a title, and made her nursery governess to the Princess.

And now I must tell you about the Princess's learning and accomplishments, for which she had such a wonderful character. Clever Angelica certainly was, but as *idle as possible*. Play at sight, indeed! she could play one or two pieces, and pretend that she had never seen them before; she could answer half-a-dozen 'Mangnal's Questions'; but then you must take care to ask the *right* ones. As for her languages, she had masters in plenty, but I doubt whether she knew more than a few phrases in each, for all her pretence; and as for her embroidery and her drawing, she showed beautiful specimens, it is true, but *who did them?*

This obliges me to tell the truth, and to do so I must go back ever so far, and tell you about the FAIRY BLACK-STICK.

3

Tells who the Fairy Blackstick was, and who were ever so many grand personages besides

BETWEEN the kingdoms of Paflagonia and Crim Tartary, there lived a mysterious personage, who was known in those countries as the Fairy Blackstick, from the ebony wand or crutch which she carried; on which she rode to the moon sometimes, or upon other excursions of business or pleasure, and with which she performed her wonders.

When she was young, and had been first taught the art of conjuring, by the necromancer, her father, she was always practising her skill, whizzing about from one kingdom to another upon her black stick, and conferring her fairy favours upon this Prince or that. She had scores of royal godchildren; turned numberless wicked people into beasts, birds, millstones, clocks, pumps, bootjacks, umbrellas, or other absurd shapes; and in a word was one of the most active and officious of the whole College of fairies.

But after two or three thousand years of this sport, I suppose Blackstick grew tired of it. Or perhaps she thought, 'What good am I doing by sending this Princess to sleep for a hundred years? by fixing a black pudding on to that booby's nose? by causing diamonds and pearls to drop from one little girl's mouth, and vipers and toads from another's? I begin to think I do as much harm as good by my performances. I might as well shut my incantations up, and allow things to take their natural course.

'There were my two young goddaughters, King Savio's wife, and Duke Padella's wife: I gave them each a present, which was to render them charming in the eyes of their husbands, and secure the affection of those gentlemen as long as they lived. What good did my Rose and my Ring do these two women? None on earth. From having all their whims indulged by their husbands, they became capricious, lazy, ill-humoured, absurdly vain, and leered, and languished, and fancied themselves irresistibly beautiful, when they were really quite old and hideous, the ridiculous creatures! They used actually to patronize me when I went to pay them a visit; – me, the Fairy Blackstick, who knows all the wisdom of the necromancers, and who could have turned them into baboons, and all their diamonds into strings of onions, by a single wave of my rod!' So she locked up her books in her cupboard, declined further magical performances, and scarcely used her wand at all except as a cane to walk about with.

So when Duke Padella's lady had a little son (the Duke was at that time only one of the principal noblemen in Crim Tartary), Blackstick, although invited to the christening, would not so much as attend; but merely sent her compliments and a silver papboat for the baby, which was really not worth a couple of guineas. About the same time the Queen of Paflagonia presented his Majesty with a son and heir; and guns were fired, the capital illuminated; and no end of feasts ordained to celebrate the young Prince's birth. It was thought the Fairy, who was asked to be his godmother, would at least have presented him with an invisible jacket, a flying horse, a Fortunatus's purse, or some other valuable token of her favour; but instead, Blackstick went up to the cradle of the child Giglio, when everybody was admiring him, and complimenting his royal papa and mamma, and said, 'My poor child, the best thing I can send you is a little *mis-*

18

fortune'; and this was all she would utter, to the disgust of Giglio's parents, who died very soon after, when Giglio's uncle took the throne, as we read in Chapter I.

In like manner, when CAVOLFIORE, King of Crim Tartary, had a christening of his only child, ROSALBA, the Fairy Blackstick, who had been invited, was not more gracious than in Prince Giglio's case. Whilst everybody was expatiating over the beauty of the darling child, and congratulating its parents, the Fairy Blackstick looked very sadly at the baby and its mother, and said, 'My good woman – (for the Fairy was very familiar, and no more minded a Queen than a washerwoman) – my good woman, these people who are following you will be the first to turn against you; and, as for this little lady, the best thing I can wish her is a *little misfortune*.' So she touched Rosalba with her black wand, looked severely at the courtiers, motioned the Queen an adieu with her hand, and sailed slowly up into the air out of the window.

When she was gone, the Court people, who had been awed and silent in her presence, began to speak. 'What an odious Fairy she is (they said) – a pretty Fairy, indeed! Why, she went to the King of Paflagonia's christening, and pretended to do all sorts of things for that family; and what has happened – the Prince, her godson, has been turned off his throne by his uncle. Would we allow our sweet Princess to be deprived of her rights by any enemy? Never, never, never, never!'

And they all shouted in a chorus, 'Never, never, never, never!'

Now, I should like to know, and how did these fine courtiers show their fidelity? One of King Cavolfiore's vassals, the Duke Padella just mentioned, rebelled against the King, who went out to chastise his rebellious subject. 'Anyone rebel against our beloved and august Monarch!' cried the courtiers; 'anyone resist *him*? Pooh! He is invincible, irresistible. He will bring home Padella a prisoner, and tie him to a donkey's tail, and drive him round the town, saying, "This is the way the great Cavolfiore treats rebels." '

The King went forth to vanquish Padella; and the poor Queen, who was a very timid, anxious creature, grew so frightened and ill, that I am sorry to say she died; leaving injunctions with her ladies to take care of the dear little Rosalba. – Of course they said they would. Of course they vowed they would die rather than any harm should happen to the Princess. At first the 'Crim Tartar Court Journal' stated that the King was obtaining great victories over the audacious rebel: then it was announced that the troops of the infamous Padella were in flight: then it was said that the royal army would soon come up with the enemy, and then – then the news came that King Cavolfiore was vanquished and slain by his Majesty, King Padella the First!

At this news, half the courtiers ran off to pay their duty to the conquering chief, and the other half ran away, laying hands on all the best articles in the palace; and poor little Rosalba was left there quite alone – quite alone; and she toddled from one room to another, crying, 'Countess! Duchess! (only she said "Tountess, Duttess," not being able to speak plain) bring me my mutton sop; my Royal Highness hungry! Tountess! Duttess!' And she went from the private apartments into the throne-room and nobody was there; and thence into the ball-room and nobody was there; and thence into the pages' room and nobody was there; and she toddled down the great staircase into the hall and nobody was there; and the door was open, and she went into the court, and into the garden, and thence into the wilderness, and thence into the forest where the wild beasts live, and was never heard of any more!

A piece of her torn mantle and one of her shoes were found in the wood in the mouths of two lioness's cubs, whom KING PADELLA and a royal hunting party shot – for he was King now, and reigned over Crim Tartary. 'So the poor little Princess is done for,' said he; 'well, what's done can't be helped. Gentlemen, let us go to luncheon!' And one of the courtiers took up the shoe and put it in his pocket. And there was an end of Rosalba!

4

How Blackstick was not asked to the Princess Angelica's christening

WHEN the Princess Angelica was born, her parents not only did not ask the Fairy Blackstick to the christening party, but gave orders to their porter, absolutely to refuse her if she called. This porter's name was Gruffanuff, and he had been selected for the post by their Royal Highnesses because he was a very tall fierce man, who could say 'Not at home' to a tradesman or an unwelcome visitor with a rudeness which frightened most such persons away. He was the husband of that Countess whose picture we have just seen, and as long as they were together they quarrelled from morning till night. Now this fellow tried his rudeness once too often, as you shall hear. For the Fairy Blackstick coming to call upon the Prince and Princess, who were actually sitting at the open drawing-room window, Gruffanuff not only denied them, but made the most *odious vulgar sign* as he was going to slam the door in the Fairy's face! 'Git away, hold Blackstick!' said he. 'I tell you, Master and Missis ain't at home to you': and he was, as we have said, *going* to slam the door.

But the Fairy, with her wand, prevented the door being shut; and Gruffanuff came out again in a fury, swearing in the most abominable way, and asking the Fairy 'whether she thought he was a going to stay at that there door hall day?'

'You *are* going to stay at that door all day and all night, and for many a long year,' the Fairy said, very majestically; and Gruffanuff, coming out of the door, straddling before it with his great calves, burst out laughing, and cried 'Ha, ha, ha! this *is* a good un! Ha – ah – what's this? Let me down – O – o – H'm!' and then he was dumb!

For, as the Fairy waved her wand over him, he felt himself rising off the ground, and fluttering up against the door, and then, as if a screw ran into his stomach, he felt a dreadful pain there, and was pinned to the door; and then his arms

flew up over his head; and his legs, after writhing about wildly, twisted under his body; and he felt cold, cold, growing over him, as if he was turning into metal; and he said, 'O – o – H'm!' and could say no more, because he was dumb.

He *was* turned into metal! He was from being *brazen, brass!* He was neither more nor less than a knocker! And there he was, nailed to the door in the blazing summer day

till he burned almost red hot; and there he was, nailed to the door all the bitter winter nights, till his brass nose was dropping with icicles. And the postman came and rapped at him, and the vulgarest boy with a letter came and hit him up against the door. And the King and Queen (Princess and Prince they were then), coming home from a walk that evening, the King said, 'Hullo, my dear! you have had a new knocker put on the door. Why, it's rather like our Porter in the face! What has become of that boozy vagabond?' And the housemaid came and scrubbed his nose with sandpaper; and once, when the Princess Angelica's little sister was born, he was tied up in an old kid glove; and another night, some *larking* young men tried to wrench him off, and put him to the most excruciating agony with a turnscrew. And then the Queen had a fancy to have the colour of the door altered, and the painters dabbed him over the mouth and eyes, and nearly choked him, as they painted him pea-green. I warrant he had leisure to repent of having been rude to the Fairy Blackstick!

As for his wife, she did not miss him; and as he was always guzzling beer at the public-house, and notoriously quarrelling with his wife, and in debt to the tradesmen, it was supposed he had run away from all these evils, and emigrated to Australia or America. And when the Prince and Princess chose to become King and Queen, they left their old house, and nobody thought of the Porter any more.

5

How Princess Angelica took a little maid

ONE day, when the Princess Angelica was quite a little girl, she was walking in the garden of the palace, with Mrs Gruffanuff, the governess, holding a parasol over her head, to keep her sweet complexion from the freckles, and Angelica was carrying a bun, to feed the swans and ducks in the royal pond.

They had not reached the duck-pond, when there came toddling up to them such a funny little girl! She had a great quantity of hair blowing about her chubby little cheeks, and looked as if she had not been washed or combed for ever so long. She wore a ragged bit of a cloak, and had only one shoe on.

'You little wretch, who let you in here?' asked Gruffanuff.

'Dive me dat bun,' said the little girl, 'me vely hungry.'

'Hungry! what is that?' asked Princess Angelica, and gave the child the bun.

'Oh, Princess!' says Gruffanuff, 'how good, how kind, how truly angelical you are! See, your Majesties,' she said to the King and Queen, who now came up, along with their nephew, Prince Giglio, 'how kind the Princess is! She met this little dirty wretch in the garden – I can't tell how she came in here, or why the guards did not shoot her dead at the gate! – and the dear darling of a Princess has given her the whole of her bun!'

'I didn't want it,' said Angelica.

'But you are a darling little angel all the same,' says the governess.

'Yes; I know I am,' said Angelica. 'Dirty little girl, don't you think I am very pretty?' Indeed, she had on the finest of little dresses and hats; and, as her hair was carefully curled, she really looked very well.

'Oh, pooty, pooty!' says the little girl, capering about, laughing, and dancing, and munching her bun; and as she ate it she began to sing, 'Oh, what fun to have a plum bun! how I wis it never was done!' At which, and her funny accent, Angelica, Giglio, and the King and Queen began to laugh very merrily.

'I can dance as well as sing,' says the little girl. 'I can dance, and I can sing, and I can do all sorts of ting.' And she ran to a flower-bed, and, pulling a few polyanthuses,

rhododendrons, and other flowers, made herself a little wreath, and danced before the King and Queen so drolly and prettily, that everybody was delighted.

'Who was your mother – who were your relations, little girl?' said the Queen.

The little girl said, 'Little lion was my brudder; great big lioness my mudder; neber heard of any udder.' And

she capered away on her one shoe, and everybody was exceedingly diverted.

So Angelica said to the Queen, 'Mamma, my parrot flew away yesterday out of its cage, and I don't care any more for any of my toys; and I think this funny little dirty child will amuse me. I will take her home, and give her some of my old frocks.'

'Oh, the generous darling!' says Gruffanuff.

'Which I have worn ever so many times, and am quite tired of,' Angelica went on; 'and she shall be my little maid. Will you come home with me, little dirty girl?'

The child clapped her hands, and said, 'Go home with you – yes! You pooty Princess! – Have a nice dinner, and wear a new dress!'

And they all laughed again, and took home the child to the palace, where, when she was washed and combed, and had one of the Princess's frocks given to her, she looked as handsome as Angelica, almost. Not that Angelica ever thought so; for this little lady never imagined that anybody in the world could be as pretty, as good, or as clever as herself. In order that the little girl should not become too proud and conceited, Mrs Gruffanuff took her old ragged mantle and one shoe, and put them into a glass box, with a card laid upon them, upon which was written, "These were the old clothes in which little BETSINDA was found when the great goodness and admirable kindness of her Royal Highness the Princess Angelica received this little outcast.' And the date was added, and the box locked up.

For a while little Betsinda was a great favourite with the Princess, and she danced, and sang, and made her little rhymes, to amuse her mistress. But then the Princess got a monkey, and afterwards a little dog, and afterwards a doll, and did not care for Betsinda any more, who became very melancholy and quiet, and sang no more funny songs, because nobody cared to hear her. And then, as she grew older, she was made a little lady's-maid to the Princess; and though she had no wages, she worked and mended, and put Angelica's hair in papers, and was never cross when scolded, and was always eager to please her mistress, and was always up early and to bed late, and at hand when wanted, and in fact became a perfect little maid. So the two girls grew up, and, when the Princess came out, Betsinda was never tired of waiting on her; and made her dresses better than the best milliner, and was useful in a hundred ways. Whilst the Princess was having her masters, Betsinda would sit and watch them; and in this way she picked up a great deal of learning; for she was always awake, though her mistress was not, and listened to the wise professors when Angelica was yawning or thinking of the next ball. And when the dancing-master came, Betsinda learned along with Angelica; and when the music-master came, she watched him, and practised the Princess's pieces when Angelica was away at balls and parties; and when the drawing-master came, she took note of all he said and did; and the same with French, Italian, and all other languages – she learned them from the teacher who came to Angelica. When the Princess was going out of an evening she would say, 'My good Betsinda, you may as well finish what I have begun.' 'Yes, Miss,' Betsinda would say, and sit down very cheerful, not to *finish* what Angelica began, but to *do* it.

For instance, the Princess would begin a head of a warrior, let us say, and when it was begun it was something like this.

But when it was done, the warrior was like this

Angelica fecit

(only handsomer still if possible), and the Princess put her
name to the drawing; and the Court and King and Queen,
and above all poor Giglio, admired the picture of all things,
and said, 'Was there ever a genius like Angelica?' So, I am
sorry to say, was it with the Princess's embroidery and other
accomplishments; and Angelica actually believed that she
did these things herself, and received all the flattery of the
Court as if every word of it was true. Thus she began to
think that there was no young woman in all the world equal
to herself, and that no young man was good enough for her.
As for Betsinda, as she heard none of these praises, she was
not puffed up by them, and being a most grateful, good-
natured girl, she was only too anxious to do everything which
might give her mistress pleasure. Now you begin to perceive
that Angelica had faults of her own, and was by no means
such a wonder of wonders as people represented her Royal
Highness to be.

6

How Prince Giglio behaved himself

AND now let us speak about Prince Giglio, the nephew of the reigning monarch of Paflagonia. It has already been stated, in page 1, that as long as he had a smart coat to wear, a good horse to ride, and money in his pocket, or rather to take out of his pocket, for he was very good-natured, my young Prince did not care for the loss of his crown and sceptre, being a thoughtless youth, not much inclined to politics or any kind of learning. So his tutor had a sinecure. Giglio would not learn classics or mathematics, and the Lord Chancellor of Paflagonia, SQUARETOSO, pulled a very long

face because the prince could not be got to study the Paflagonian laws and constitution; but, on the other hand, the
King's gamekeepers and huntsmen found the Prince an apt
pupil; the dancing-master pronounced that he was a most
elegant and assiduous scholar; the First Lord of the Billiard
Table gave the most flattering reports of the Prince's skill;
so did the Groom of the Tennis Court; and as for the Captain
of the Guard and Fencing Master, the *valiant* and *veteran*

Count KUTASOFF HEDZOFF, he avowed that since he ran
the General of Crim Tartary, the dreadful Grumbuskin,
through the body, he never had encountered so expert a
swordsman as Prince Giglio.

I hope you do not imagine that there was any impropriety
in the Prince and Princess walking together in the palace

garden, and because Giglio kissed Angelica's hand in a polite manner. In the first place they are cousins; next, the Queen is walking in the garden too (you cannot see her, for she happens to be behind that tree), and her Majesty always wished that Angelica and Giglio should marry: so did Giglio: so did Angelica sometimes, for she thought her cousin very handsome, brave, and good-natured: but then you know she was so clever and knew so many things, and poor Giglio knew nothing, and had no conversation. When they looked at the stars, what did Giglio know of the heavenly bodies? Once, when on a sweet night in a balcony where they were stand-

34

ing, Angelica said, 'There is the Bear.' 'Where?' says Giglio. 'Don't be afraid, Angelica! if a dozen bears come, I will kill them rather than they shall hurt you.' 'Oh, you silly creature!' says she: 'you are very good, but you are not very wise.' When they looked at the flowers, Giglio was utterly unacquainted with botany, and had never heard of Linnaeus. When the butterflies passed, Giglio knew nothing about them, being as ignorant of entomology as I am of algebra. So you see, Angelica, though she liked Giglio pretty well, despised him on account of his ignorance. I think she probably valued *her own learning* rather too much; but to think too well of one's self is the fault of people of all ages and both sexes. Finally, when nobody else was there, Angelica liked her cousin well enough.

King Valoroso was very delicate in health, and withal so fond of good dinners (which were prepared for him by his French cook, Marmitonio), that it was supposed he could not live long. Now the idea of anything happening to the King struck the artful Prime Minister and the designing old lady-in-waiting with terror. For, thought Glumboso and the Countess, 'when Prince Giglio marries his cousin and comes

to the throne, what a pretty position we shall be in, whom he dislikes, and who have always been unkind to him. We shall lose our places in a trice; Gruffanuff will have to give up all the jewels, laces, snuff-boxes, rings, and watches which belonged to the Queen, Giglio's mother; and Glumboso will be forced to refund two hundred and seventeen thousand millions, nine hundred and eighty-seven thousand, four hundred and thirty-nine pounds, thirteen shillings, and sixpence halfpenny, money left to Prince Giglio by his poor dear father.' So the Lady of Honour and the Prime Minister hated Giglio because they had done him a wrong; and these unprincipled people invented a hundred cruel stories about poor Giglio, in order to influence the King, Queen, and Princess against him; how he was so ignorant that he could not spell the commonest words, and actually wrote Valoroso Valloroso, and spelt Angelica with two l's; how he drank a great deal too much wine at dinner, and was always idling in the stables with the grooms; how he owed ever so much money at the pastrycook's and the haberdasher's; how he used to go to sleep at church; how he was fond of playing cards with the pages. So did the Queen like playing cards; so did the King go to sleep at church, and eat and drink too much; and, if Giglio owed a trifle for tarts, who owed him two hundred and seventeen thousand millions, nine hundred and eighty-seven thousand, four hundred and thirty-nine pounds, thirteen shillings, and sixpence halfpenny, I should like to know? Detractors and tale-bearers (in my humble opinion) had much better look at *home*. All this back-biting and slandering had effect upon Princess Angelica, who began to look coldly on her cousin, then to laugh at him and scorn him for being so stupid, then to sneer at him for having vulgar associates; and at Court balls, dinners, and so forth, to treat him so unkindly that poor Giglio became quite ill, took to his bed, and sent for the doctor.

His Majesty King Valoroso, as we have seen, had his own reasons for disliking his nephew; and as for those innocent readers who ask why? – I beg (with the permission of their dear parents) to refer them to Shakespeare's pages, where they will read why King John disliked Prince Arthur. With the Queen, his royal but weak-minded aunt, when Giglio was out of sight he was out of mind. While she had her whist and her evening parties, she cared for little else.

I dare say *two villains*, who shall be nameless, wished Doctor Pildrafto, the Court Physician, had killed Giglio right out, but he only bled and physicked him so severely, that the Prince was kept to his room for several months, and grew as thin as a post.

Whilst he was lying sick in this way, there came to the Court of Paflagonia a famous painter, whose name was Tomaso Lorenzo, and who was Painter in Ordinary to the King of Crim Tartary, Paflagonia's neighbour. Tomaso Lorenzo painted all the Court, who were delighted with his works; for even Countess Gruffanuff looked young and Glumboso good-humoured in his pictures. 'He flatters very much,' some people said. 'Nay!' says Princess Angelica, 'I am above flattery, and I think he did not make my picture handsome enough. I can't bear to hear a man of genius unjustly cried down, and I hope my dear papa will make Lorenzo a knight of his Order of the Cucumber.'

The Princess Angelica, although the courtiers vowed her Royal Highness could draw so *beautifully* that the idea of her taking lessons was absurd, yet chose to have Lorenzo for a teacher, and it was wonderful, *as long as she painted in his studio*, what beautiful pictures she made! Some of the performances were engraved for the Book of Beauty: others were sold for enormous sums at Charity Bazaars. She wrote the *signatures* under the drawings no doubt, but I think I know who did the pictures – this artful painter, who had come with other designs on Angelica than merely to teach her to draw.

One day, Lorenzo showed the Princess a portrait of a young man in armour, with fair hair and the loveliest blue eyes, and an expression at once melancholy and interesting.

'Dear Signor Lorenzo, who is this?' asked the Princess. 'I never saw anyone so handsome,' says Countess Gruffanuff (the old humbug).

'That,' said the painter, 'that, madam, is the portrait of my august young master, his Royal Highness Bulbo, Crown Prince of Crim Tartary, Duke of Acroceraunia, Marquis of Poluphloisoio, and Knight Grand Cross of the Order of the Pumpkin. That is the Order of the Pumpkin glittering on his manly breast, and received by his Royal Highness from his august father, his Majesty King PADELLA I, for his gallantry at the battle of Rimbombamento, when he slew with his own princely hand the King of Ograria and two hundred and eleven giants of the two hundred and eighteen who formed the King's body-guard. The remainder were destroyed by the brave Crim Tartary army after an obstinate combat, in which the Crim Tartars suffered severely.'

What a Prince! thought Angelica: so brave – so calm-looking – so young – what a hero!

'He is as accomplished as he is brave,' continued the Court Painter. 'He knows all languages perfectly: sings deliciously: plays every instrument: composes operas which have been acted a thousand nights running at the Imperial Theatre of Crim Tartary, and danced in a ballet there before the King and Queen; in which he looked so beautiful, that his cousin, the lovely daughter of the King of Circassia, died for love of him.'

'Why did he not marry the poor Princess?' asked Angelica, with a sigh.

'Because they were *first cousins*, Madam, and the clergy forbid these unions,' said the Painter. 'And, besides, the young Prince had given his royal heart *elsewhere*.'

'And to whom?' asked her Royal Highness.

'I am not at liberty to mention the Princess's name,' answered the Painter.

'But you may tell me the first letter of it,' gasped out the Princess.

'That your Royal Highness is at liberty to guess,' says Lorenzo.

'Does it begin with a Z?' asked Angelica.

The painter said it wasn't a Z; then she tried a Y; then an X; then a W, and went so backwards through almost the whole alphabet.

When she came to D, and it wasn't D, she grew very much excited; when she came to C, and it wasn't C, she was still more nervous; when she came to B, *and it wasn't B*, 'O, dearest Gruffanuff,' she said, 'lend me your smelling-bottle!' and, hiding her head in the Countess's shoulder, she faintly whispered, 'Ah, Signor, can it be A?'

'It was A; and though I may not, by my Royal Master's orders, tell your Royal Highness the Princess's name, whom he fondly, madly, devotedly, rapturously loves, I may show you her portrait,' says the slyboots: and leading the Princess up to a gilt frame, he drew a curtain which was before it.

O goodness, the frame contained A LOOKING GLASS! and Angelica saw her own face!

7

How Giglio and Angelica had a quarrel

THE Court Painter of his Majesty the King of Crim Tartary returned to that monarch's dominions, carrying away a number of sketches which he had made in the Paflagonian capital (you know, of course, my dears, that the name of that capital is Blombodinga); but the most charming of all his pieces was a portrait of the Princess Angelica, which all the Crim Tartar nobles came to see. With this work the King was so delighted, that he decorated the Painter with his Order of the Pumpkin (sixth class), and the artist became Sir Tomaso Lorenzo, K.P., thenceforth.

King Valoroso also sent Sir Tomaso his Order of the Cucumber, besides a handsome order for money, for he painted the King, Queen, and principal nobility while at Blombodinga, and became all the fashion, to the perfect rage of all the artists in Paflagonia, where the King used to point to the portrait of Prince Bulbo, which Sir Tomaso had left behind him, and say, 'Which among you can paint a picture like that?'

It hung in the royal parlour over the royal sideboard, and Princess Angelica could always look at it as she sat making the tea. Each day it seemed to grow handsomer and handsomer, and the Princess grew so fond of looking at it, that she would often spill the tea over the cloth, at which her father and mother would wink and wag their heads, and say to each other, 'Aha! we see how things are going.'

In the meanwhile poor Giglio lay upstairs very sick in his

chamber, though he took all the doctor's horrible medicines like a good young lad; as I hope *you* do, my dears, when you are ill and mamma sends for the medical man. And the only person who visited Giglio (besides his friend the captain of the guard, who was almost always busy or on parade), was little Betsinda the housemaid, who used to do his bedroom and sitting-room out, bring him his gruel, and warm his bed.

When the little housemaid came to him in the morning and evening, Prince Giglio used to say, 'Betsinda, Betsinda, how is the Princess Angelica?'

And Betsinda used to answer, 'The Princess is very well, thank you, my Lord.' And Giglio would heave a sigh, and think, if Angelica were sick I am sure *I* should not be very well.

Then Giglio would say, 'Betsinda, has the Princess Angelica asked for me today?' And Betsinda would answer, 'No, my Lord, not today'; or, 'she was very busy practising the piano when I saw her'; or, 'she was writing invitations for an evening party, and did not speak to me': or make some excuse or other, not strictly consonant with truth: for Betsinda was such a good-natured creature, that she strove to do everything to prevent annoyance to Prince Giglio, and even brought him up roast chicken and jellies from the kitchen (when the Doctor allowed them, and Giglio was getting better), saying, 'that the Princess had made the jelly or the bread sauce, with her own hands, on purpose for Giglio.'

When Giglio heard this he took heart, and began to mend immediately; and gobbled up all the jelly, and picked the last bone of the chicken – drumsticks, merry-thought, side-bones, back, pope's-nose, and all – thanking his dear Angelica: and he felt so much better the next day, that he dressed and went downstairs, where, whom should he meet but Angelica going into the drawing-room. All the covers were off the chairs, the chandeliers taken out of the bags, the damask curtains uncovered, the work and things carried away, and the handsomest albums on the tables. Angelica had her hair in papers: in a word, it was evident there was going to be a party.

'Heavens, Giglio!' cries Angelica: '*you* here in such a dress! What a figure you are!'

'Yes, dear Angelica, I am come downstairs, and feel so well today, thanks to the *fowl* and the *jelly*.'

'What do I know about fowls and jellies, that you allude to them in that rude way?' says Angelica.

'Why, didn't – didn't you send them, Angelica dear?' says Giglio.

'I send them indeed! Angelica dear! No, Giglio dear,' says she, mocking him, '*I* was engaged in getting the rooms ready for his Royal Highness the Prince of Crim Tartary, who is coming to pay my papa's Court a visit.'

'The – Prince – of – Crim – Tartary!' Giglio said, aghast.

'Yes, the Prince of Crim Tartary,' says Angelica, mocking him. 'I dare say you never heard of such a country. What *did* you ever hear of? You don't know whether Crim Tartary is on the Red Sea or on the Black Sea, I dare say.'

'Yes, I do, it's on the Red Sea,' says Giglio, at which the Princess burst out laughing at him, and said, 'O you ninny! You are so ignorant, you are really not fit for society! You know nothing but about horses and dogs, and are only fit to dine in a mess-room with my Royal Father's heaviest dragoons. Don't look so surprised at me, sir: go and put your best clothes on to receive the Prince, and let me get the drawing-room ready.'

Giglio said, 'O, Angelica, Angelica, I didn't think this of you. *This* wasn't your language to me when you gave me this ring, and I gave you mine in the garden, and you gave me that k—'

But what k was we never shall know, for Angelica, in a rage, cried, 'Get out, you saucy, rude creature! How dare you remind me of your rudeness? As for your little trumpery twopenny ring, there, sir, there!' And she flung it out of the window.

'It was my mother's marriage ring,' cries Giglio.

'*I* don't care whose marriage ring it was,' cries Angelica. 'Marry the person who picks it up if she's a woman, you shan't marry *me*. And give me back *my* ring. I've no patience with people who boast about the things they give away! *I* know who'll give me much finer things than you ever gave me. A beggarly ring indeed, not worth five shillings!'

Now Angelica little knew that the ring which Giglio had given her was a fairy ring: if a man wore it, it made all the women in love with him; if a woman, all the gentlemen. The Queen, Giglio's mother, quite an ordinary looking person, was admired immensely whilst she wore this ring, and her husband was frantic when she was ill. But when she called her little Giglio to her, and put the ring on his finger, King Savio did not seem to care for his wife so much any more, but transferred all his love to little Giglio. So did everybody love him as long as he had the ring; but when, as quite a child, he gave it to Angelica, people began to love and admire *her*; and Giglio, as the saying is, played only second fiddle.

'Yes,' says Angelica, going on in her foolish ungrateful way, '*I* know who'll give me much finer things than your beggarly little pearl nonsense.'

'Very good, Miss! You may take back your ring, too!' says Giglio, his eyes flashing fire at her, and then, as if his eyes had been suddenly opened, he cried out, 'Ha! what does this mean? Is *this* the woman I have been in love with all my life? Have I been such a ninny as to throw away my regard upon *you*? Why – actually – yes – you are a little crooked!'

'O, you wretch!' cries Angelica.

'And, upon my conscience, you – you squint a little.'

'Eh!' cries Angelica.

'And your hair is red – and you are marked with the small-pox – and what? you have three false teeth – and one leg shorter than the other!'

'You brute, you brute, you!' Angelica screamed out: and as she seized the ring with one hand, she dealt Giglio one, two, three smacks on the face, and would have pulled the hair off his head had he not started laughing, and crying:

'O dear me, Angelica, don't pull out *my* hair, it hurts! You might remove a great deal of *your own*, as I perceive, without scissors or pulling at all. O, ho, ho! ha, ha, ha! he, he, he!'

And he nearly choked himself with laughing, and she with rage, when, with a low bow, and dressed in his Court habit, Count Gambabella, the first lord-in-waiting, entered and said, 'Royal Highnesses! Their Majesties expect you in the Pink Throne-room, where they await the arrival of the Prince of CRIM TARTARY.'

8

How Gruffanuff picked the fairy ring up, and Prince Bulbo came to court

PRINCE BULBO'S arrival had set all the Court in a flutter: everybody was ordered to put his or her best clothes on: the footmen had their gala liveries; the Lord Chancellor his new wig; the Guards their last new tunics; and Countess Gruffanuff you may be sure was glad of an opportunity of decorating *her* old person with her finest things. She was walking through the court of the Palace on her way to wait upon their Majesties, when she spied something glittering on the pavement, and bade the boy in buttons who was holding up her train, to go and pick up the article shining yonder. He was an ugly little wretch, in some of the late groom-porter's old clothes cut down, and much too tight for him; and yet, when he had taken up the ring (as it turned out to be), and was carrying it to his mistress, she thought he looked like a little Cupid. He gave the ring to her; it was a trumpery little thing enough, but too small for any of her old knuckles, so she put it into her pocket.

'O, mum!' says the boy, looking at her, 'how, how beautiful you do look, mum, today, mum!'

'And you, too, Jacky,' she was going to say; but, looking down at him – no, he was no longer good-looking at all but only the carroty-haired little Jacky of the morning. However, praise is welcome from the ugliest of men or boys, and Gruffanuff, bidding the boy hold up her train, walked on in high good-humour. The guards saluted her with peculiar

47

respect. Captain Hedzoff, in the ante-room, said, 'My dear madam, you look like an angel today.' And so, bowing and smirking, Gruffanuff went in and took her place behind her Royal Master and Mistress, who were in the throne-room, awaiting the Prince of Crim Tartary. Princess Angelica sat at their feet, and behind the King's chair stood Prince Giglio, looking very savage.

The Prince of Crim Tartary made his appearance, attended by Baron Sleibootz, his chamberlain, and followed by a page, carrying the most beautiful crown you ever saw! He was dressed in his travelling costume, and his hair was a little in disorder. 'I have ridden three hundred miles since breakfast,' said he, 'so eager was I to behold the Prin – the Court and august family of Paflagonia, and I could not wait one minute before appearing in your Majesties' presences.'

Giglio, from behind the throne, burst out into a roar of contemptuous laughter; but all the Royal party, in fact, were so flurried, that they did not hear this little outbreak. 'Your R.H. is welcome in any dress,' says the King. 'Glumboso, a chair for his Royal Highness.'

'Any dress his Royal Highness wears *is* a Court dress,' says Princess Angelica, smiling graciously.

'Ah! but you should see my other clothes,' said the Prince. 'I should have had them on, but that stupid carrier has not brought them. Who's that laughing?'

It was Giglio laughing. 'I was laughing,' he said, 'because you said just now that you were in such a hurry to see the Princess, that you could not wait to change your dress; and now you say you come in those clothes because you have no others.'

'And who are you?' says Prince Bulbo, very fiercely.

'My father was King of this country, and I am his only son, Prince!' replies Giglio, with equal haughtiness.

'Ha!' said the King and Glumboso, looking very flurried; but the former, collecting himself, said, 'Dear Prince Bulbo, I forgot to introduce to your Royal Highness my dear nephew, his Royal Highness Prince Giglio! Know each other! Embrace each other! Giglio, give His Royal Highness

your hand!' and Giglio, giving his hand, squeezed poor
Bulbo's until the tears ran out of his eyes. Glumboso now
brought a chair for the Royal visitor, and placed it on the
platform on which the King, Queen, and Prince were seated;
but the chair was on the edge of the platform, and as Bulbo
sat down, it toppled over, and he with it, rolling over and
over, and bellowing like a bull. Giglio roared still louder at
this disaster, but it was with laughter; so did all the Court
when Prince Bulbo got up; for though when he entered the
room he appeared not very ridiculous, as he stood up from
his fall for a moment, he looked so exceedingly plain and
foolish, that nobody could help laughing at him. When he
had entered the room, he was observed to carry a rose in his
hand, which fell out of it as he tumbled.

'My rose! my rose!' cried Bulbo; and his chamberlain
dashed forward and picked it up, and gave it to the Prince,
who put it in his waistcoat. Then people wondered why they
had laughed; there was nothing particularly ridiculous in
him. He was rather short, rather stout, rather red-haired,
but, in fine, for a Prince not so bad.

So they sat and talked, the royal personages together, the
Crim Tartar officers with those of Paflagonia – Giglio very
comfortable with Gruffanuff behind the throne. He looked
at her with such tender eyes, that her heart was all in a
flutter. 'Oh, dear Prince,' she said, 'how could you speak
so haughtily in presence of their Majesties? I protest I
thought I should have fainted.'

'I should have caught you in my arms,' said Giglio looking raptures.

'Why were you so cruel to Prince Bulbo, dear Prince?' says
Gruff.

'Because I hate him,' says Gil.

'You are jealous of him, and still love poor Angelica,' cries
Gruffanuff, putting her handkerchief to her eyes.

'I did, but I love her no more!' Giglio cried. 'I despise her! Were she heiress to twenty thousand thrones, I would despise her and scorn her. But why speak of thrones? I have lost mine. I am too weak to recover it – I am alone, and have no friend.'

'Oh, say not so, dear Prince!' says Gruffanuff.

'Besides,' says he, 'I am so happy here *behind the throne*, that I would not change my place, no, not for the throne of the world!'

'What are you two people chattering about there?' says the Queen, who was rather good-natured, though not over-burthened with wisdom. 'It is time to dress for dinner. Giglio, show Prince Bulbo to his room. Prince, if your clothes have not come, we shall be very happy to see you as you are.' But when Prince Bulbo got to his bedroom, his luggage was there and unpacked; and the hairdresser coming in, cut and curled him entirely to his own satisfaction; and

when the dinner-bell rang, the royal company had not to
wait above five-and-twenty minutes until Bulbo appeared,
during which time the King, who could not bear to wait,
grew as sulky as possible. As for Giglio, he never left Madam
Gruffanuff all this time, but stood with her in the embrasure
of a window, paying her compliments. At length the Groom
of the Chambers announced his Royal Highness the Prince
of Crim Tartary! and the noble company went into the royal
dining-room. It was quite a small party; only the King and

Queen, the Princess, whom Bulbo took out, the two Princes, Countess Gruffanuff, Glumboso the Prime Minister, and Prince Bulbo's chamberlain. You may be sure they had a very good dinner – let every boy or girl think of what he or she likes best, and fancy it on the table.*

The Princess talked incessantly all dinner-time to the Prince of Crimea, who ate an immense deal too much, and never took his eyes off his plate, except when Giglio, who was carving a goose, sent a quantity of stuffing and onion sauce into one of them. Giglio only burst out a-laughing as the Crimean Prince wiped his shirt-front and face with his scented pocket-handkerchief. He did not make Prince Bulbo any apology. When the Prince looked at him, Giglio would not look that way. When Prince Bulbo said, 'Prince Giglio, may I have the honour of taking a glass of wine with you?' Giglio *wouldn't* answer. All his talk and his eyes were for Countess Gruffanuff, who you may be sure was pleased with Giglio's attentions – the vain old creature! When he was not complimenting her, he was making fun of Prince Bulbo, so loud that Gruffanuff was always tapping him with her fan, and saying, 'O you satirical Prince! O fie, the Prince will hear!' 'Well, I don't mind,' says Giglio, louder still. The King and Queen luckily did not hear; for her Majesty was a little deaf, and the King thought so much about his own dinner, and, besides, made such a dreadful noise, hobgobbling in eating it, that he heard nothing else. After dinner, his Majesty and the Queen went to sleep in their armchairs.

This was the time when Giglio began his tricks with Prince Bulbo, plying that young gentleman with port, sherry, madeira, champagne, marsala, cherry brandy, and pale ale, of all of which Master Bulbo drank without stint. But in

* Here a very pretty game may be played by all the children saying what they like best for dinner.

plying his guest, Giglio was obliged to drink himself, and, I am sorry to say, took more than was good for him, so that the young men were very noisy, rude, and foolish when they joined the ladies after dinner; and dearly did they pay for that imprudence, as now, my darlings, you shall hear!

Bulbo went and sat by the piano, where Angelica was playing and singing, and he sang out of tune, and he upset the coffee when the footman brought it, and he laughed out of place, and talked absurdly, and fell asleep and snored horridly. Booh, the nasty pig! But as he lay there stretched on the pink satin sofa, Angelica still persisted in thinking him the most beautiful of human beings. No doubt the magic rose which Bulbo wore, caused this infatuation on Angelica's part; but is she the first young woman who has thought a silly fellow charming?

Giglio must go and sit by Gruffanuff, whose old face he too every moment began to find more lovely. He paid the most outrageous compliments to her: There never was such a darling – Older than he was? – Fiddle-de-dee! He would marry her – he would having nothing but her!

To marry the heir to the throne! Here was a chance! The artful hussy actually got a sheet of paper, and wrote upon it, 'This is to give notice that I, Giglio, only son of Savio, King of Paflagonia hereby promise to marry the charming and virtuous Barbara Griselda Countess Gruffanuff, and widow of the late Jenkins Gruffanuff, Esq.'

'What is it you are writing? you charming Gruffy!' says Giglio, who was lolling on the sofa, by the writing-table.

'Only an order for you to sign, dear Prince, for giving coals and blankets to the poor, this cold weather. Look! the King and Queen are both asleep, and your Royal Highness's order will do.'

So Giglio, who was very good-natured, as Gruffy well knew, signed the order immediately; and, when she had it in her pocket, you may fancy what airs she gave herself. She was ready to flounce out of the room before the Queen herself, as now she was the wife of the *rightful* King of Paflagonia! She would not speak to Glumboso, whom she thought a brute, for depriving her *dear husband* of the crown! And when candles came, and she had helped to undress the Queen and Princess, she went into her own room, and actually practised, on a sheet of paper, 'Griselda Paflagonia', 'Barbara Regina', 'Griselda Barbara, Paf. Reg.', and I don't know what signatures besides, against the day when she should be Queen, forsooth!

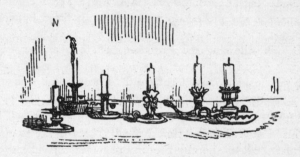

9

How Betsinda got the warming-pan

LITTLE BETSINDA came in to put Gruffanuff's hair in papers; and the Countess was so pleased, that, for a wonder, she complimented Betsinda. 'Betsinda!' she said, 'you dressed my hair very nicely today; I promised you a little present. Here are five sh – no, here is a pretty little ring, that I picked – that I have had some time.' And she gave Betsinda the ring she had picked up in the court. It fitted Betsinda exactly.

'It's like the ring the Princess used to wear,' says the maid.

'No such thing,' says Gruffanuff, 'I have had it this ever so long. There – tuck me up quite comfortable; and now, as it's a very cold night (the snow was beating in at the window), you may go and warm dear Prince Giglio's bed, like a good girl, and then you may unrip my green silk, and then you can just do me up a little cap for the morning, and then you can mend that hole in my silk stocking, and then you can go to bed, Betsinda. Mind, I shall want my cup of tea at five o'clock in the morning.'

'I suppose I had best warm both the young gentlemen's beds, ma'am,' says Betsinda.

Gruffanuff, for reply, said, 'Hau-au-ho! – Grau-haw-hoo! – Hong-hrho!' In fact, she was snoring sound asleep.

Her room, you know, is next to the King and Queen, and the Princess is next to them. So pretty Betsinda went away for the coals to the kitchen, and filled the royal warming-pan.

Now, she was a very kind, merry, civil, pretty girl; but there must have been something very captivating about her this evening, for all the women in the servants' hall began to scold and abuse her. The housekeeper said she was a pert, stuck-up thing: the upper-housemaid asked, how dare she wear such ringlets and ribbons, it was quite improper! The cook (for there was a woman-cook as well as a man-cook) said to the kitchen-maid that *she* never could see anything in that creetur: but as for the men, every one of them, Coachman, John, Buttons the page, and Monsieur, the Prince of Crim Tartary's valet, started up, and said –

'My eyes!'
'O mussey!'
'O jemmany!' } 'What a pretty girl Betsinda is!'
'O ciel!'

'Hands off; none of your impertinence, you vulgar, low people!' says Betsinda, walking off with her pan of coals. She heard the young gentlemen playing at billiards as she went upstairs: first to Prince Giglio's bed, which she warmed, and then to Prince Bulbo's room.

He came in just as she had done; and as soon as he saw her, 'O! O! O! O! O! O! what a beyou – oo – ootiful creature you are! You angel – you peri – you rose-bud, let me be thy bulbul – thy Bulbo, too! Fly to the desert, fly with me! I never saw a young gazelle to glad me with its dark blue eye that had eyes like thine. Thou nymph of beauty, take, take this young heart. A truer never did itself sustain within a soldier's waistcoat. Be mine! Be mine! Be Princess of Crim Tartary! My Royal father will approve our union: and, as for that little carroty-haired Angelica, I do not care a fig for her any more.'

'Go away, your Royal Highness, and go to bed, please,' said Betsinda, with the warming-pan.

But Bulbo said, 'No, never, till thou swearest to be mine,

thou lovely, blushing, chamber-maid divine! Here, at thy feet, the Royal Bulbo lies, the trembling captive of Betsinda's eyes.'

And he went on, making himself so *absurd and ridiculous*, that Betsinda, who was full of fun, gave him a touch with the warming-pan, which, I promise you, made him cry 'O-o-o-o!' in a very different manner.

Prince Bulbo made such a noise that Prince Giglio, who heard him from the next room, came in to see what was the matter. As soon as he saw what was taking place, Giglio, in a fury, rushed on Bulbo, kicked him in the rudest manner up to the ceiling, and went on kicking him till his hair was quite out of curl.

The rivals

Poor Betsinda did not know whether to laugh or to cry; the kicking certainly must hurt the Prince, but then he looked so droll! When Giglio had done knocking him up and down to the ground, and whilst he went into a corner rubbing himself, what do you think Giglio does? He goes down on his own knees to Betsinda, takes her hand, begs her to accept his heart, and offers to marry her that moment. Fancy Betsinda's condition, who had been in love with the Prince ever since she first saw him in the palace garden, when she was quite a little child.

'Oh, divine Betsinda!' says the Prince, 'how have I lived fifteen years in thy company without seeing thy perfections? What woman in all Europe, Asia, Africa, and America, nay, in Australia, only it is not yet discovered, can presume to be thy equal? Angelica? Pish! Gruffanuff? Phoo! The Queen? Ha, ha! Thou art my Queen. Thou art the real Angelica, because thou art really angelic.'

'Oh, Prince! I am but a poor chamber-maid,' says Betsinda, looking, however, very much pleased.

'Didst thou not tend me in my sickness, when all forsook me?' continues Giglio. 'Did not thy gentle hand smooth my pillow, and bring me jelly and roast chicken?'

'Yes, dear Prince, I did,' says Betsinda, 'and I sewed your Royal Highness's shirt-buttons on too, if you please, your Royal Highness,' cries this artless maiden.

When poor Prince Bulbo, who was now madly in love with Betsinda, heard this declaration, when he saw the unmistakable glances which she flung upon Giglio, Bulbo began to cry bitterly, and tore quantities of hair out of his head, till it all covered the room like so much tow.

Betsinda had left the warming-pan on the floor while the princes were going on with their conversation, and as they began now to quarrel and be very fierce with one another, she thought proper to run away.

'You great big blubbering booby, tearing your hair in the corner there; of course you will give me satisfaction for insulting Betsinda. *You* are to kneel down at Princess Giglio's knees and kiss her hand!'

'She's not Princess Giglio!' roars out Bulbo. 'She shall be Princess Bulbo, no other shall be Princess Bulbo.'

'You are engaged to my cousin!' bellows out Giglio.

'I hate your cousin,' says Bulbo.

'You shall give me satisfaction for insulting her!' cries Giglio in a fury.

'I'll have your life.'

'I'll run you through.'

'I'll cut your throat.'

'I'll blow your brains out.'

'I'll knock your head off.'

'I'll send a friend to you in the morning.'

'I'll send a bullet into you in the afternoon.'

'We'll meet again,' says Giglio, shaking his fist in Bulbo's face; and seizing up the warming-pan, he kissed it, because, forsooth, Betsinda had carried it, and rushed downstairs. What should he see on the landing but his Majesty talking to Betsinda, whom he called by all sorts of fond names. His Majesty had heard a row in the building, so he stated, and smelling something burning, had come out to see what the matter was.

'It's the young gentlemen smoking, perhaps, sir,' says Betsinda.

'Charming chamber-maid,' says the King (like all the rest of them), 'never mind the young men! Turn thy eyes on a middle-aged autocrat, who has been considered not ill-looking in his time.'

'Oh, sir! what will her Majesty say?' cries Betsinda.

'Her Majesty!' laughs the monarch. 'Her Majesty be hanged. Am I not Autocrat of Paflagonia? Have I not blocks, ropes, axes, hangmen – ha? Runs not a river by my palace wall? Have I not sacks to sew up wives withal? Say but the word, that thou wilt be mine own – your mistress straight-way in a sack is sewn, and thou the sharer of my heart and throne.'

When Giglio heard these atrocious sentiments, he forgot the respect usually paid to Royalty, lifted up the warming-pan, and knocked down the King as flat as a pancake; after

which, Master Giglio took to his heels and ran away, and Betsinda went off screaming, and the Queen, Gruffanuff, and the Princess, all came out of their rooms. Fancy their feelings on beholding their husband, father, sovereign, in this posture!

10

How King Valoroso was in a dreadful passion

As soon as the coals began to burn him, the King came to himself and stood up. 'Ho! my captain of the guards!' his Majesty exclaimed, stamping his royal feet with rage. O piteous spectacle! the King's nose was bent quite crooked by the blow of Prince Giglio! His Majesty ground his teeth with rage. 'Hedzoff,' he said, taking a death warrant out of his dressing-gown pocket, 'Hedzoff, good Hedzoff, seize upon

the Prince. Thou'lt find him in his chamber two pair up. But now he dared, with sacrilegious hand, to strike the sacred night-cap of a king, Hedzoff, and floor me with a warming-pan! Away, no more demur, the villain dies! See it be done, or else – h'm! – ha! – h'm! mind thine own eyes!' and followed by the ladies, and lifting up the tails of his dressing-gown, the King entered his own apartment.

Captain Hedzoff was very much affected, having a sincere love for Giglio. 'Poor, poor Giglio!' he said, the tears rolling over his manly face, and dripping down his moustachios; 'My noble young Prince, is it my hand must lead thee to death?'

'Lead him to fiddlestick, Hedzoff,' said a female voice. It was Gruffanuff, who had come out in her dressing-gown when she heard the noise – 'The King said you were to hang the Prince. Well, hang the Prince.'

'I don't understand you,' says Hedzoff, who was not a very clever man.

'You Gaby! he didn't say *which* Prince,' says Gruffanuff.

'No; he didn't say which, certainly,' said Hedzoff.

'Well then, take Bulbo, and hang *him!*'

When Captain Hedzoff heard this, he began to dance about for joy. 'Obedience is a soldier's honour,' says he. 'Prince Bulbo's head will do capitally,' and he went to arrest the Prince the very first thing next morning.

He knocked at the door. 'Who's there?' says Bulbo. 'Captain Hedzoff? Step in, pray, my good Captain; I'm delighted to see you; I have been expecting you.'

'Have you?' says Hedzoff.

'Sleibootz, my Chamberlain, will act for me,' says the Prince.

'I beg your Royal Highness's pardon, but you will have to act for yourself, and it's a pity to wake Baron Sleibootz.'

The Prince Bulbo still seemed to take the matter very coolly. 'Of course, Captain,' says he, 'you are come about that affair with Prince Giglio?'

'Precisely,' says Hedzoff, 'that affair of Prince Giglio.'

'Is it to be pistols, or swords, Captain?' asks Bulbo. 'I'm a pretty good hand with both, and I'll do for Prince Giglio as sure as my name is my Royal Highness Prince Bulbo.'

'There's some mistake, my Lord,' says the Captain. 'The business is done with *axes* among us.'

'Axes? That's sharp work,' says Bulbo. 'Call my Chamberlain, he'll be my second, and in ten minutes, I flatter myself you'll see Master Giglio's head off his impertinent shoulders. I'm hungry for his blood. Hoo-oo, aw!' and he looked as savage as an ogre.

'I beg your pardon, sir, but by this warrant, I am to take you prisoner, and hand you over to – to the executioner.'

'Pooh, pooh, my good man! – Stop, I say – ho! – hulloa!'
was all that this luckless Prince was enabled to say, for
Hedzoff's guards seizing him, tied a handkerchief over his
mouth and face, and carried him to the place of execution.

The King, who happened to be talking to Glumboso, saw
him pass, and took a pinch of snuff, and said, 'So much for
Giglio. Now let's go to breakfast.'

The Captain of the Guard handed over his prisoner to the
Sheriff, with the fatal order,

AT SIGHT CUT OFF THE BEARER'S HEAD.

VALOROSO XXIV

'It's a mistake,' says Bulbo, who did not seem to understand the business in the least.

'Poo – poo – pooh,' says the Sheriff. 'Fetch Jack Ketch instantly. Jack Ketch!'

And poor Bulbo was led to the scaffold, where an executioner with a block and a tremendous axe was always ready in case he should be wanted.

But we must now revert to Giglio and Betsinda.

11

What Gruffanuff did to Giglio and Betsinda

GRUFFANUFF, who had seen what had happened with the King, and knew that Giglio must come to grief, got up very early the next morning, and went to devise some plans for rescuing her darling husband, as the silly old thing insisted on calling him. She found him walking up and down the garden, thinking of a rhyme for Betsinda (*tinder* and *winda* were all he could find), and indeed having forgotten all about the past evening, except that Betsinda was the most lovely of beings.

'Well, dear Giglio,' says Gruff.

'Well, dear Gruffy,' says Giglio, only *he* was quite satirical.

'I have been thinking, darling, what you must do in this scrape. You must fly the country for a while.'

'What scrape? – fly the country? Never without her I love, Countess,' says Giglio.

'No, she will accompany you, dear Prince,' she says, in her most coaxing accents. 'First, we must get the jewels belonging to our royal parents, and those of her and his present Majesty. Here is the key, duck; they are all yours, you know, by right, for you are the rightful King of Paflagonia, and your wife will be the rightful Queen.'

'Will she?' says Giglio.

'Yes; and having got the jewels, go to Glumboso's apartment, where, under his bed, you will find sacks containing money to the amount of £217,000,000,987,439 13s. 6½d., all belonging to you, for he took it out of your royal father's room on the day of his death. With this we will fly.'

69

'*We* will fly?' says Giglio.

'Yes, you and your bride – your affianced love – your Gruffy!' says the Countess, with a languishing leer.

'*You* my bride!' says Giglio. 'You, you hideous old woman!'

'Oh, you, you wretch! didn't you give me this paper promising marriage?' cries Gruff.

'Get away, you old goose! I love Betsinda, and Betsinda only!' And in a fit of terror he ran from her as quickly as he could.

'He! he! he!' shrieks out Gruff; 'a promise is a promise, if there are laws in Paflagonia! And as for that monster, that wretch, that fiend, that ugly little vixen – as for that upstart, that ingrate, that beast Betsinda, Master Giglio will have no little difficulty in discovering her whereabouts. He may look very long before finding *her*, I warrant. He little knows that Miss Betsinda is –'

Is – what? Now, you shall hear. Poor Betsinda got up at five in the winter's morning to bring her cruel mistress her tea; and instead of finding her in a good humour, found Gruffy as cross as two sticks. The Countess boxed Betsinda's ears half-a-dozen times whilst she was dressing; but as poor little Betsinda was used to this kind of treatment, she did not feel any special alarm. 'And now,' says she, 'when her Majesty rings her bell twice, I'll trouble you, miss, to attend.'

So when the Queen's bell rang twice, Betsinda came to her Majesty and made a pretty little curtsey. The Queen, the Princess, and Gruffanuff were all three in the room. As soon as they saw her they began.

'You wretch!' says the Queen.

'You vulgar thing!' says the Princess.

'You beast!' says Gruffanuff.

'Get out of my sight!' says the Queen.

'Go away with you, do!' says the Princess.

'Quit the premises!' says Gruffanuff.

Alas! and woe is me! very lamentable events had occurred to Betsinda that morning, and all in consequence of that fatal warming-pan business of the previous night. The King had offered to marry her; of course her Majesty the Queen was jealous: Bulbo had fallen in love with her; of course Angelica was furious: Giglio was in love with her, and O what a fury Gruffy was in!

'Take off that
$\begin{Bmatrix} \text{cap} \\ \text{petticoat} \\ \text{gown} \end{Bmatrix}$
I gave you,' they said, all at once,

and began tearing the clothes off poor Betsinda.

'How dare you flirt with { the King?' Prince Bulbo?' Prince Giglio?' } cried the Queen, the Princess, and Countess.

'Give her the rags she wore when she came into the house, and turn her out of it!' cries the Queen.

'Mind she does not go with *my* shoes on, which I lent her so kindly,' says the Princess; and indeed the Princess's shoes were a great deal too big for Betsinda.

'Come with me, you filthy hussy!' and taking up the Queen's poker, the cruel Gruffanuff drove Betsinda into her room.

The Countess went to the glass box in which she had kept Betsinda's old cloak and shoe this ever so long, and said, 'Take those rags, you little beggar creature, and strip off everything belonging to honest people, and go about your business'; and she actually tore off the poor little delicate thing's back almost all her things, and told her to be off out of the house.

Poor Betsinda huddled the cloak round her back, on which were embroidered the letters PRIN .... ROSAL ... and then came a great rent.

As for the shoe, what was she to do with one poor little tootsey sandal? the string was still to it, so she hung it round her neck.

'Won't you give me a pair of shoes to go out in the snow, mum, if you please, mum?' cried the poor child.

'No, you wicked beast!' says Gruffanuff, driving her along with the poker – driving her down the cold stairs – driving her through the cold hall – flinging her out into the cold street, so that the knocker itself shed tears to see her!

But a kind Fairy made the soft snow warm for her little feet, and she wrapped herself up in the ermine of her mantle, and was gone!

'And now let us think about breakfast,' says the greedy Queen.

'What dress shall I put on mamma? the pink or the pea-green?' says Angelica. 'Which do you think the dear Prince will like best?'

'Mrs V.!' sings out the King from his dressing-room, 'let us have sausages for breakfast! Remember we have Prince Bulbo staying with us!'

And they all went to get ready.

Nine o'clock came, and they were all in the breakfast-room, and no Prince Bulbo as yet. The urn was hissing and humming: the muffins were smoking – such a heap of muffins! the eggs were done, there was a pot of raspberry jam, and coffee, and a beautiful chicken and tongue on the side-table. Marmitonio the cook brought in the sausages. O, how nice they smelt!

'Where is Bulbo?' said the King. 'John, where is his Royal Highness?'

John said he had a-took up his Roilighnessesses shaving-water, and his clothes and things, and he wasn't in his room, which he sposed his Royliness was just stepped hout.

'Stepped out before breakfast in the snow! Impossible!' says the King, sticking his fork into a sausage. 'My dear, take one. Angelica, won't you have a saveloy?' The Princess took one, being very fond of them; and at this moment Glumboso entered with Captain Hedzoff, both looking very much disturbed. 'I am afraid your Majesty –' cries Glumboso. 'No business before breakfast, Glum!' says the King. 'Breakfast first, business next. Mrs V., some more sugar!'

'Sire, I am afraid if we wait till after breakfast it will be too late,' says Glumboso. 'He – he – he'll be hanged at half-past nine.'

'Don't talk about hanging and spóil my breakfast, you unkind vulgar man you,' cries the Princess. 'John, some mustard. Pray who is to be hanged?'

'Sire, it is the Prince,' whispers Glumboso to the King.

'Talk about business after breakfast, I tell you!' says his Majesty, quite sulky.

'We shall have a war, Sire, depend on it,' says the Minister. 'His father, King Padella . . .'

'His father, King *who*?' says the King. 'King Padella is not Giglio's father. My brother, King Savio, was Giglio's father.'

'It's Prince Bulbo they are hanging, Sire, not Prince Giglio,' says the Prime Minister.

'You told me to hang the Prince, and I took the ugly one,' says Hedzoff. 'I didn't, of course, think your Majesty intended to murder your own flesh and blood!'

The King for all reply flung the plate of sausages at Hedzoff's head. The Princess cried out Hee-karee-karee! and fell down in a fainting fit.

'Turn the cock of the urn upon her Royal Highness,' said the King, and the boiling water gradually revived her. His Majesty looked at his watch, compared it by the clock in the parlour, and by that of the church in the square opposite; then he wound it up; then he looked at it again. 'The great question is,' says he, 'am I fast or am I slow? If I'm slow, we may as well go on with breakfast. If I'm fast, why, there is just the possibility of saving Prince Bulbo. It's a doosid awkward mistake, and upon my word, Hedzoff, I have the greatest mind to have you hanged too.'

'Sire, I did but my duty; a soldier has but his orders. I didn't expect after forty-seven years of faithful service that my sovereign would think of putting me to a felon's death!'

'A hundred thousand plagues upon you! Can't you see that while you are talking my Bulbo is being hung?' screamed the Princess.

'By Jove! she's always right, that girl, and I'm so absent,' says the King, looking at his watch again. 'Ha! Hark, there go the drums! What a doosid awkward thing though!'

'O Papa, you goose! Write the reprieve, and let me run with it,' cries the Princess – and she got a sheet of paper, and pen and ink, and laid them before the King.

'Confound it! Where are my spectacles?' the Monarch exclaimed. 'Angelica! Go up into my bedroom, look under my pillow, not your mamma's; there you'll see my keys. Bring them down to me, and – Well, well! what impetuous things these girls are!' Angelica was gone, and had run up panting to the bedroom, and found the keys, and was back again before the King had finished a muffin. 'Now love,' says he, 'you must go all the way back for my desk, in which my spectacles are. If you *would* but have heard me out. . . . Be hanged to her. There she is off again. Angelica! AN-GELICA!' When his Majesty called in his *loud* voice, she knew she must obey, and came back.

'My dear, when you go out of a room, how often have I told you, *shut the door*. That's a darling. That's all.' At last the keys and the desk and the spectacles were got, and the King mended his pen, and signed his name to a reprieve, and Angelica ran with it as swift as the wind. 'You'd better stay, my love, and finish the muffins. There's no use going. Be sure it's too late. Hand me over that raspberry jam, please,' said the Monarch. 'Bong! Bawong! There goes the half hour. I knew it was.'

Angelica ran, and ran, and ran, and ran. She ran up Fore Street, and down High Street, and through the Market-place, and down to the left, and over the bridge, and up the blind alley, and back again, and round by the Castle, and so along by the Haberdasher's on the right, opposite the lamp-post, and round the square, and she came – she came to the *Execution place*, where she saw Bulbo laying his head on the block!!! The executioner raised his axe, but at that moment the Princess came panting up and cried Reprieve. 'Reprieve!' screamed the Princess. 'Reprieve!' shouted all

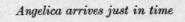

Angelica arrives just in time

the people. Up the scaffold stairs she sprang, with the agility of a lighter of lamps; and flinging herself in Bulbo's arms, regardless of all ceremony, she cried out, 'O my Prince! my lord! my love! my Bulbo! Thine Angelica has been in time to save thy precious existence, sweet rose-bud; to prevent thy being nipped in thy young bloom! Had aught befallen thee, Angelica too had died, and welcomed death that joined her to her Bulbo.'

'H'm! there's no accounting for tastes,' said Bulbo, look-ing so very much puzzled and uncomfortable, that the Princess, in tones of tenderest strain, asked the cause of his disquiet.

'I tell you what it is, Angelica,' said he, 'since I came here, yesterday, there has been such a row, and disturbance, and quarrelling, and fighting, and chopping of heads off, and the deuce to pay, that I am inclined to go back to Crim Tartary.'

'But with me as thy bride, my Bulbo! Though wherever thou art is Crim Tartary to me, my bold, my beautiful, my Bulbo!'

'Well, well, I suppose we must be married,' says Bulbo. 'Doctor, you came to read the Funeral Service – read the Marriage Service, will you? What must be, must. That will satisfy Angelica, and then, in the name of peace and quiet-ness, do let us go back to breakfast.'

Bulbo had carried a rose in his mouth all the time of the dismal ceremony. It was a fairy rose, and he was told by his mother that he ought never to part with it. So he had kept it between his teeth, even when he laid his poor head upon the block, hoping vaguely that some chance would turn up in his favour. As he began to speak to Angelica, he forgot about the rose, and of course it dropped out of his mouth. The romantic Princess instantly stooped and seized it. 'Sweet rose!' she exclaimed, 'that bloomed upon my Bulbo's lip, never, never will I part from thee!' and she placed it in her bosom. And you know Bulbo *couldn't* ask her to give the rose back again. And they went to breakfast; and as they walked, it appeared to Bulbo that Angelica became more exquisitely lovely every moment.

He was frantic until they were married; and now, strange to say, it was Angelica who didn't care about him! He knelt down, he kissed her hand, he prayed and begged; he cried with admiration; while she for her part said she really thought they might wait; it seemed to her he was not hand-some any more – no, not at all, quite the reverse; and not clever, no, very stupid; and not well bred, like Giglio; no, on the contrary, dreadfully vul –

What, I cannot say, for King Valoroso roared out '*Pooh*, stuff!' in a terrible voice. 'We will have no more of this shilly-shallying! Call the Archbishop, and let the Prince and Princess be married off-hand!'

So, married they were, and I am sure for my part I trust they will be happy.

12

How Betsinda fled, and what became of her

BETSINDA wandered on and on, till she passed through the town gates, and so on the great Crim Tartary road, the very way on which Giglio too was going. 'Ah!' thought she, as the diligence passed her, of which the conductor was blowing a delightful tune on his horn, 'how I should like to be on that coach!' But the coach and the jingling horses were very soon gone. She little knew who was in it, though very likely she was thinking of him all the time.

Then came an empty cart, returning from market; and the driver being a kind man, and seeing such a very pretty girl trudging along the road with bare feet, most good-naturedly gave her a seat. He said he lived on the confines of the forest, where his old father was a woodman, and, if she liked, he would take her so far on her road. All roads were the same to little Betsinda, so she very thankfully took this one.

And the carter put a cloth round her bare feet, and gave her some bread and cold bacon, and was very kind to her. For all that she was very cold and melancholy. When after travelling on and on, evening came, and all the black pines were bending with snow, and there, at last, was the comfortable light beaming in the woodman's windows; and so they arrived, and went into his cottage. He was an old man, and had a number of children, who were just at supper, with nice hot bread-and-milk, when their elder brother arrived with the cart. And they jumped and clapped their hands; for they were good children; and he had brought them toys from the

81

town. And when they saw the pretty stranger, they ran to her, and brought her to the fire, and rubbed her poor little feet, and brought her bread-and-milk.

'Look, Father!' they said to the old woodman, 'look at this poor girl, and see what pretty cold feet she has. They are as white as our milk! And look and see what an odd cloak she has, just like the bit of velvet that hangs up in our cupboard, and which you found that day the little cubs were killed by King Padella, in the forest! And look, why, bless us all! she has got round her neck just such another little shoe as that you brought home, and have shown us so often – a little blue velvet shoe!'

'What,' said the old woodman, 'What is all this about a shoe and a cloak?'

And Betsinda explained that she had been left, when quite a little child, at the town with this cloak and this shoe. And the persons who had taken care of her had – had been angry with her, for no fault, she hoped, of her own. And they had sent her away with her old clothes – and here, in fact, she was. She remembered having been in a forest – and perhaps it was a dream – it was so very odd and strange – having lived in a cave with lions there; and, before that, having lived in a very, very fine house, as fine as the King's, in the town.

When the woodman heard this, he was so astonished, it was quite curious to see how astonished he was. He went to

his cupboard, and took out of a stocking a five-shilling piece of King Cavolfiore, and vowed it was exactly like the young woman. And then he produced the shoe and the piece of velvet which he had kept so long, and compared them with the things which Betsinda wore. In Betsinda's little shoe was written, 'Hopkins, maker to the Royal Family'; so in the other shoe was written, 'Hopkins, maker to the Royal Family'. In the inside of Betsinda's piece of cloak was embroidered, 'PRIN ROSAL'; in the other piece of cloak was embroidered, 'CESS BA. No. 246'. So that when put together you read, 'PRINCESS ROSALBA. No. 246'.

On seeing this, the dear old woodman fell down on his knees, saying: 'O my princess, O my gracious royal lady, O my rightful Queen of Crim Tartary – I hail thee – I acknowledge thee – I do thee homage!' And in token of his fealty, he rubbed his venerable nose three times on the ground, and put the Princess's foot on his head.

'Why,' said she, 'my good woodman, you must be a noble-man of my royal father's Court!' For in her lowly retreat, and under the name of Betsinda, HER MAJESTY, ROSALBA, Queen of Crim Tartary, had read of the customs of all foreign Courts and nations.

'Marry, indeed am I, my gracious liege – the poor Lord Spinachi, once – the humble woodman these fifteen years syne. Ever since the tyrant Padella (may ruin overtake the treacherous knave!) dismissed me from my post of First Lord.'

'First Lord of the Toothpick and Joint Keeper of the Snuff-box? I mind me! Thou heldest these posts under our royal Sire. They are restored to thee, Lord Spinachi! I make thee knight of the second class of our Order of the Pumpkin (the first class being reserved for crowned heads alone). Rise, Marquis of Spinachi!' And with indescribable majesty, the Queen, who had no sword handy, waved the pewter spoon with which she had been taking her bread-and-milk, over the bald head of the old nobleman, whose tears absolutely made a puddle on the ground, and whose dear children went to bed that night Lords and Ladies Bartolomeo, Ubaldo, Catarina, and Ottavia degli Spinachi!

The acquaintance HER MAJESTY showed with the his-tory, and *noble families* of her empire, was wonderful. 'The House of Broccoli should remain faithful to us,' she said; 'they were ever welcome at our Court. Have the Articiocchi, as was their wont, turned to the Rising Sun? The family of Sauerkraut must sure be with us – they were ever welcome in the halls of King Cavolfiore.' And so she went on enumer-ating quite a list of the nobility and gentry of Crim Tartary, so admirably had her Majesty profited by her studies while in exile.

The old Marquis of Spinachi said he could answer for them all; that the whole country groaned under Padella's tyranny, and longed to return to its rightful sovereign; and late as it was, he sent his children, who knew the forest well, to summon this nobleman and that; and when his eldest son, who had been rubbing the horse down and giving him his supper, came into the house for his own, the Marquis told him to put his boots on, and a saddle on the mare, and ride hither and thither to such and such people.

When the young man heard who his companion in the cart had been, he too knelt down and put her royal foot on his head, he too bedewed the ground with his tears; he was frantically in love with her, as everybody now was who saw her: so were the young Lords Bartolomeo and Ubaldo, who punched each other's little heads out of jealousy: and so, when they came from east and west at the summons of the Marquis degli Spinachi, were the Crim Tartar Lords who still remained faithful to the House of Cavolfiore. They were such very old gentlemen for the most part, that her Majesty never suspected their absurd passion, and went among them quite unaware of the havoc her beauty was causing, until an old blind Lord who had joined her party, told her what the truth was; after which, for fear of making the people too much in love with her, she always wore a veil. She went about privately, from one nobleman's castle to another: and they visited amongst themselves again, and had meetings, and composed proclamations and counter-proclamations, and distributed all the best places of the kingdom amongst one another, and selected who of the opposition party should be executed when the Queen came to her own. And so in about a year they were ready to move.

The party of Fidelity was in truth composed of very feeble old fogies for the most part; they went about the country waving their old swords and flags, and calling 'God save the Queen!' and King Padella happening to be absent upon an invasion, they had their own way for a little, and to be sure the people were very enthusiastic whenever they saw the Queen; otherwise the vulgar took matters very quietly, for they said, as far as they could recollect, they were pretty well as much taxed in Cavolfiore's time, as now in Padella's.

13

How Queen Rosalba came to the castle of the bold Count Hogginarmo

HER MAJESTY, having indeed nothing else to give, made all her followers Knights of the Pumpkin, and Marquises, Earls, and Baronets; and they had a little court for her, and made her a little crown of gilt paper, and a robe of cotton velvet; and they quarrelled about the places to be given away in her court, and about rank and precedence and dignities; you can't think how they quarrelled! The poor Queen was very tired of her honours before she had had them a month, and I dare say sighed sometimes even to be a lady's-maid again. But we must all do our duty in our respective stations, so the Queen resigned herself to perform hers.

We have said how it happened that none of the Usurper's troops came out to oppose this Army of Fidelity: it pottered along as nimbly as the gout of the principal commanders allowed: it consisted of twice as many officers as soldiers: and at length passed near the estates of one of the most powerful noblemen of the country, who had not declared for the Queen, but of whom her party had hopes, as he was always quarrelling with King Padella.

When they came close to his park gates, this nobleman sent to say he would wait upon her Majesty: he was a most powerful warrior, and his name was Count Hogginarmo, whose helmet it took two strong pages to carry. He knelt down before her and said, 'Madam and liege lady! it becomes the great nobles of the Crimean realm to show every outward

sign of respect to the wearer of the Crown, whoever that may
be. We testify to our own nobility in acknowledging yours.
The bold Hogginarmo bends the knee to the first of the
aristocracy of his country.'

Rosalba said, 'The bold Count of Hogginarmo was uncommonly kind.' But she felt afraid of him, even while he
was kneeling, and his eyes scowled at her from between his
whiskers, which grew up to them.

'The first Count of the Empire, madam,' he went on,
'salutes the Sovereign. The Prince addresses himself to the
not more noble lady! Madam, my hand is free, and I offer
it, and my heart and my sword to your service! My three
wives lie buried in my ancestral vaults. The third perished
but a year since; and this heart pines for a consort! Deign
to be mine, and I swear to bring to your bridal table the
head of King Padella, the eyes and nose of his son Prince
Bulbo, the right hand and ears of the usurping Sovereign of
Paflagonia, which country shall thenceforth be an apanage
to your – to *our* Crown! Say yes; Hogginarmo is not accustomed to be denied. Indeed I cannot contemplate the possibility of a refusal; for frightful will be the result; dreadful
the murders; furious the devastations; horrible the tyranny;
tremendous the tortures, misery, taxation, which the people
of this realm will endure, if Hogginarmo's wrath be aroused!
I see consent in your Majesty's lovely eyes – their glances fill
my soul with rapture!'

'O, Sir!' Rosalba said, withdrawing her hand in great
fright. 'Your Lordship is exceedingly kind; but I am sorry
to tell you that I have a prior attachment to a young gentleman by the name of – Prince – Giglio – and never – never can
marry anyone but him.'

Who can describe Hogginarmo's wrath at this remark?
Rising up from the ground, he ground his teeth so that fire
flashed out of his mouth, from which at the same time issued

remarks and language, so *loud, violent, and improper*, that this pen shall never repeat them! 'R-r-r-r-r – Rejected! Fiends and perdition! The bold Hogginarmo rejected! All the world shall hear of my rage; and you, Madam, you above all shall rue it!' And he rushed away, his whiskers streaming in the wind.

Her Majesty's Privy Council was in a dreadful panic when they saw Hogginarmo issue from the royal presence in such a towering rage – a panic which the events justified. They marched off from Hogginarmo's park very crest-fallen; and in another half-hour they were met by that rapacious chieftain with a few of his followers, who cut, slashed, charged, whacked, banged and pommelled amongst them, took the Queen prisoner, and drove the Army of Fidelity to I don't know where.

Poor Queen! Hogginarmo, her conqueror, would not condescend to see her. 'Get a horse-van!' he said to his grooms, 'clap the hussy into it, and send her, with my compliments, to his Majesty King Padella.'

Along with his lovely prisoner, Hogginarmo sent a letter full of servile compliments and loathsome flatteries to King Padella, for whose life, and that of his royal family, the *hypocritical humbug* pretended to offer the most fulsome prayers. And Hogginarmo promised speedily to pay his humble homage at his august master's throne, of which he begged leave to be counted the most loyal and constant defender. Such a *wary* old *bird* as King Padella was not to be caught by Master Hogginarmo's *chaff*, and we shall hear presently how the tyrant treated his upstart vassal. No, no; depend on't, two such rogues do not trust one another.

So this poor Queen was laid in the straw like Margery Daw, and driven along in the dark ever so many miles to the Court, where King Padella had now arrived, having vanquished all his enemies, murdered most of them, and brought some of the richest into captivity with him for the purpose of torturing them and finding out where they had hidden their money.

Rosalba heard their shrieks and groans in the dungeon in which she was thrust; a most awful black hole, full of bats, rats, mice, toads, frogs, mosquitoes, bugs, fleas, serpents, and every kind of horror. No light was let into it, otherwise the gaolers might have seen her and fallen in love with her, as an owl that lived up in the roof of the tower did, and a cat, you know, who can see in the dark, and having set its green eyes on Rosalba, never would be got to go back to the turnkey's wife to whom it belonged. And the toads in the dungeon came and kissed her feet, and the vipers wound round her neck and arms, and never hurt her, so charming was this poor Princess in the midst of her misfortunes.

At last, after she had been kept in this place *ever so long*, the door of the dungeon opened, and the terrible KING PADELLA came in.

But what he said and did must be reserved for another Chapter, as we must now back to Prince Giglio.

King Padella

14

What became of Giglio

THE idea of marrying such an old creature as Gruffanuff, frightened Prince Giglio so, that he ran up to his room, packed his trunks, fetched in a couple of porters, and was off to the diligence office in a twinkling.

It was well that he was so quick in his operations, did not dawdle over his luggage, and took the early coach, for as soon as the mistake about Prince Bulbo was found out, that cruel Glumboso sent up a couple of policemen to Prince Giglio's room, with orders that he should be carried to Newgate, and his head taken off before twelve o'clock. But the coach was out of the Paflagonian dominions before two o'clock; and I daresay the express that was sent after Prince Giglio did not ride very quick, for many people in Paflagonia had a regard for Giglio, as the son of their old sovereign; a Prince who, with all his weaknesses, was very much better than his brother the reigning, usurping, lazy, careless, passionate, tyrannical, reigning monarch. That Prince busied himself with the balls, fêtes, masquerades, hunting parties, and so forth, which he thought proper to give on occasion of his daughter's marriage to Prince Bulbo; and let us trust was not sorry in his own heart that his brother's son had escaped the scaffold.

It was very cold weather, and the snow was on the ground, and Giglio, who gave his name as simple Mr Giles, was very glad to get a comfortable place on the coupé of the diligence, where he sat with the conductor and another gentleman. At the first stage from Blombodinga, as they stopped to change horses, there came up to the diligence a very ordinary, vulgar-looking woman, with a bag under her arm, who asked for a place. All the inside places were taken, and the young woman was informed that if she wished to travel, she must go upon the roof; and the passenger inside with Giglio (a rude person, I should think), put his head out of the window, and said, 'Nice weather for travelling outside! I wish you a

pleasant journey, my dear.' The poor woman coughed very much, and Giglio pitied her. 'I will give up my place to her,' says he, 'rather than she should travel in the cold air with that horrid cough.' On which the vulgar traveller said, '*You'd* keep her warm, I am sure, if it's a *muff* she wants.' On which Giglio pulled his nose, boxed his ears, hit him in the eye, and gave this vulgar person a warning never to call him *muff* again.

Then he sprang up gaily on to the roof of the diligence, and made himself very comfortable in the straw. The vulgar traveller got down only at the next station, and Giglio took his place again, and talked to the person next to him. She appeared to be a most agreeable, well-informed, and entertaining female. They travelled together till night, and she gave Giglio all sorts of things out of the bag which she carried, and which indeed seemed to contain the most wonderful collection of articles. He was thirsty – out there came a pint bottle of Bass's pale ale, and a silver mug! Hungry – she took out a cold fowl, some slices of ham, bread, salt, and a most delicious piece of cold plum-pudding, and a little glass of brandy afterwards.

As they travelled, this plain-looking, queer woman talked to Giglio on a variety of subjects, in which the poor Prince showed his ignorance as much as she did her capacity. He owned, with many blushes, how ignorant he was; on which the lady said, 'My dear Gigl – my good Mr Giles, you are a young man, and have plenty of time before you. You have nothing to do but to improve yourself. Who knows but that you may find use for your knowledge some day? When – when you may be wanted at home, as some people may be.'

'Good Heavens, madam!' says he, 'do you know me?'

'I know a number of funny things,' says the lady. 'I have been at some people's christenings, and turned away from other folks' doors. I have seen some people spoilt by good fortune, and others, as I hope, improved by hardship. I advise you to stay at the town where the coach stops for the night. Stay there and study, and remember your old friend to whom you were kind.'

'And who is my old friend?' asked Giglio.

'When you want anything,' says the lady, 'look in this bag, which I leave to you as a present, and be grateful to –'

'To whom, madam?' says he.

'To the Fairy Blackstick,' says the lady, flying out of the window. And when Giglio asked the conductor if he knew where the lady was?

'What lady?' says the man; 'there has been no lady in this coach, except the old woman, who got out at the last stage.' And Giglio thought he had been dreaming. But there was the bag which Blackstick had given him lying on his lap; and when he came to the town he took it in his hand and went into the inn.

They gave him a very bad bedroom, and Giglio, when he woke in the morning, fancying himself in the Royal Palace at home, called, 'John, Charles, Thomas! My chocolate – my dressing-gown – my slippers'; but nobody came. There was no bell, so he went and bawled out for the waiter on the top of the stairs.

The landlady came up, looking – looking like this –

'What are you a hollaring and a bellaring for here, young man?' says she.

'There's no warm water – no servants; my boots are not even cleaned.'

'He, he! Clean 'em yourself,' says the landlady. 'You young students give yourselves pretty airs. I never heard such impudence.'

'I'll quit the house this instant,' says Giglio.

'The sooner the better, young man. Pay your bill and be off. All my rooms is wanted for gentlefolks, and not for such as you.'

'You may well keep the Bear Inn,' said Giglio. 'You should have yourself painted as the sign.'

The landlady of the Bear went away *growling*. And Giglio returned to his room, where the first thing he saw was the fairy bag lying on the table, which seemed to give a little hop as he came in. 'I hope it has some breakfast in it,' says Giglio, 'for I have only a very little money left.' But on opening the bag, what do you think was there? A blacking-brush and a pot of Warren's jet, and on the pot was written,

'Poor young men their boots must black:
Use me and cork me and put me back.'

So Giglio laughed and blacked his boots, and put back the brush and the bottle into the bag.

When he had done dressing himself, the bag gave another little hop, and he went to it and took out –

1. A tablecloth and a napkin.
2. A sugar-basin full of the best loaf sugar.
4, 6, 8, 10. Two forks, two teaspoons, two knives, and a
   pair of sugar-tongs, and a butter-knife, all marked G.
11, 12, 13. A teacup, saucer, and slop-basin.
14. A jug full of delicious cream.
15. A canister with black tea and green.
16. A large tea-urn and boiling water.
17. A saucepan, containing three eggs nicely done.
18. A quarter of a pound of best Epping butter.
19. A brown loaf.

And if he hadn't enough now for a good breakfast, I
should like to know who ever had one?

Giglio, having had his breakfast, popped all the things
back into the bag, and went out looking for lodgings. I forgot to say that this celebrated university town was called
Bosforo.

He took a modest lodging opposite the Schools, paid his
bill at the inn, and went to his apartment with his trunk,
carpet-bag, and not forgetting, we may be sure, his *other* bag.

When he opened his trunk, which the day before he had
filled with his best clothes, he found it contained only books.
And in the first of them which he opened there was written –

'Clothes for the back, books for the head;
Read, and remember them when they are read.'

And in his bag, when Giglio looked in it, he found a student's
cap and gown, a writing-book full of paper, an inkstand,
pens, and a Johnson's dictionary, which was very useful to
him, as his spelling had been sadly neglected.

So he sat down and worked away, very, very hard for a
whole year, during which 'Mr Giles' was quite an example
to all the students in the University of Bosforo. He never got
into any riots or disturbances. The Professors all spoke well

of him, and the students liked him, too; so that, when at examination, he took all the prizes, viz.:

The Spelling Prize	The French Prize
The Writing Prize	The Arithmetic Prize
The History Prize	The Latin Prize
The Catechism Prize	The Good Conduct Prize,

all his fellow students said, 'Hurray! Hurray for Giles! Giles is the boy – the student's joy! Hurray for Giles!' And he brought quite a quantity of medals, crowns, books, and tokens of distinction home to his lodgings.

One day after the Examinations, as he was diverting himself at a coffee house, with two friends – (Did I tell you that in his bag, every Saturday night, he found just enough to pay his bills, with a guinea over, for pocket-money! Didn't I tell you? Well, he did, as sure as twice twenty makes forty-five) – he chanced to look in the 'Bosforo Chronicle', and read off quite easily (for he could spell, read, and write the longest words now) the following –

'ROMANTIC CIRCUMSTANCE. – One of the most extraordinary adventures that we have ever heard has set the neighbouring country of Crim Tartary in a state of great excitement.

'It will be remembered that when the present revered sovereign of Crim Tartary, his Majesty King *Padella*, took possession of the throne, after having vanquished, in the terrific battle of Blunderbusco, the late King *Cavolfiore*, that Prince's only child, the Princess Rosalba, was not found in the royal palace, of which King Padella took possession, and, it was said, had strayed into the forest (being abandoned by all her attendants), where she had been eaten up by those ferocious lions, the last pair of which were captured some time since, and brought to the Tower, after killing several hundred persons.

'His Majesty King Padella, who has the kindest heart in the world, was grieved at the accident which had occurred to the harmless little Princess, for whom his Majesty's known benevolence would certainly have provided a fitting establishment. But her death seemed to be certain. The mangled remains of a cloak, and a little shoe, were found in the forest, during a hunting party, in which the intrepid sovereign of Crim Tartary slew two of the lions' cubs with his own spear. And these interesting relics of an innocent little creature were carried home and kept by their finder, the Baron Spinachi, formerly an officer in Cavolfiore's household. The Baron was disgraced in consequence of his known legitimist opinions, and has lived for some time in the humble capacity of a wood-cutter, in a forest on the outskirts of the Kingdom of Crim Tartary.

'Last Tuesday week Baron Spinachi and a number of gentlemen attached to the former dynasty, appeared in arms, crying, "God save Rosalba, the First Queen of Crim Tartary!" and surrounding a lady whom report describes as *"beautiful exceedingly"*. Her history *may* be authentic, *is* certainly most romantic.

'The personage calling herself Rosalba states that she was brought out of the forest, fifteen years since, by a lady in a car drawn by dragons (this account is certainly *improbable*), that she was left in the Palace Garden of Blombodinga, where her Royal Highness the Princess Angelica, now married to his Royal Highness Bulbo, Crown Prince of Crim Tartary, found the child, and, with *that elegant benevolence* which has always distinguished the heiress of the throne of Paflagonia, gave the little outcast a *shelter and a home*! Her parentage not being known, and her garb very humble, the foundling was educated in the Palace in a menial capacity, under the name of *Betsinda*.

'She did not give satisfaction, and was dismissed, carrying

with her, certainly, part of a mantle and a shoe, which she had on when first found. According to her statement she quitted Blombodinga about a year ago, since which time she has been with the Spinachi family. On the very same morning the Prince Giglio, nephew to the King of Paflagonia, a young Prince whose character for *talent* and *order* were, to say truth, *none of the highest*, also quitted Blombodinga, and has not been since heard of!'

'What an extraordinary story!' said Smith and Jones, two young students, Giglio's especial friends.

'Ha! what is this?' Giglio went on, reading –

'SECOND EDITION, EXPRESS. – We hear that the troop under Baron Spinachi has been surrounded, and utterly routed, by General Count Hogginarmo, and the *soi-disant* Princess is sent a prisoner to the capital.

'UNIVERSITY NEWS. – Yesterday, at the Schools, the distinguished young student, Mr Giles, read a Latin oration, and was complimented by the Chancellor of Bosforo, Dr Prugnaro, with the highest University honour – the wooden spoon.'

'Never mind that stuff,' says *Giles*, greatly disturbed. 'Come home with me, my friends. Gallant Smith! intrepid Jones! friends of my studies – partakers of my academic toils – I have that to tell shall astonish your honest minds.'

'Go it, old boy!' cried the impetuous Smith.

'Talk away, my buck!' says Jones, a lively fellow.

With an air of indescribable dignity, Giglio checked their natural, but no more seemly, familiarity. 'Jones, Smith, my good friends,' said the PRINCE, 'disguise is henceforth useless; I am no more the humble student Giles, I am the descendant of a royal line.'

'*Atavis edite regibus*, I know, old co –' cried Jones, he was going to say old cock, but a flash from THE ROYAL EYE again awed him.

To Arms!

'Friends,' continued the Prince, 'I am that Giglio, I am in fact, Paflagonia. Rise, Smith, and kneel not in the public street. Jones, thou true heart! My faithless uncle, when I was a baby, filched from me that brave crown my father left me, bred me, all young and careless of my rights, like unto hapless Hamlet, Prince of Denmark; and had I any thoughts about my wrongs, soothed me with promises of near redress. I should espouse his daughter young Angelica; we two indeed should reign in Paflagonia. His words were false – false as Angelica's heart! – false as Angelica's hair, colour, front teeth! She looked with her skew eyes upon young Bulbo, Crim Tartary's stupid heir, and she preferred him. 'Twas then I turned my eyes upon Betsinda – Rosalba, as she now is. And I saw in her the blushing sum of all perfection; the pink of maiden modesty; the nymph that my fond heart had ever woo'd in dreams,' &c., &c.

(I don't give this speech, which was very fine, but very long; and though Smith and Jones knew nothing about the circumstances, my dear reader does, so I go on.)

The Prince and his young friends hastened home to his apartment, highly excited by the intelligence, as no doubt by the *royal narrator's* admirable manner of recounting it, and they ran up to his room where he had worked so hard at his books.

On his writing-table was his bag, grown so long that the Prince could not help remarking it. He went to it, opened it, and what do you think he found in it?

A splendid long, gold-handled, red-velvet-scabbarded, cut-and-thrust sword, and on the sheath was embroidered 'ROSALBA FOR EVER!'

He drew out the sword, which flashed and illuminated the whole room, and called out 'Rosalba for ever!' Smith and Jones following him, but quite respectfully this time, and taking the time from his Royal Highness.

And now his trunk opened with a sudden ping, and out there came three ostrich feathers in a gold crown, surrounding a beautiful shining steel helmet, a cuirass, a pair of spurs, finally a complete suit of armour.

The books on Giglio's shelves were all gone. Where there had been some great dictionaries, Giglio's friend found two pairs of jackboots labelled 'Lieutenant Smith', '— Jones, Esq.', which fitted them to a nicety. Besides, there were helmets, back and breast plates, swords, &c., just like in Mr G. P. R. James's novels; and that evening three cavaliers might have been seen issuing from the gates of Bosforo, in whom the porters, &c., never thought of recognizing the young Prince and his friends.

They got horses at a livery-stable keeper's, and never drew bridle until they reached the last town on the frontier before you come to Crim Tartary. Here, as their animals were tired, and the cavaliers hungry, they stopped and refreshed at an hostel. I could make a chapter of this if I were like some writers, but I like to cram my measure tight down, you see, and give you a great deal for your money, and in a word they had some bread and cheese and ale upstairs on the balcony of the inn. As they were drinking, drums and trumpets sounded nearer and nearer, the market-place was filled with soldiers, and his Royal Highness looking forth, recognized the Paflagonian banners, and the Paflagonian national air which the bands were playing.

The troops all made for the tavern at once, and as they came up Giglio exclaimed, on beholding their leader, 'Whom do I see? Yes! No! It is, it is! Phoo! No, it can't be! Yes! It is my friend, my gallant faithful veteran, Captain Hedzoff! Ho! Hedzoff! Knowest thou not thy Prince, thy Giglio? Good Corporal, methinks we once were friends. Ha, Sergeant, an my memory serves me right, we have had many a bout at singlestick.'

'I'faith, we have, a many, good my Lord,' says the Sergeant.

'Tell me, what means this mighty armament,' continued his Royal Highness from the balcony, 'and whither march my Paflagonians?'

Hedzoff's head fell. 'My Lord,' he said, 'we march as the allies of great Padella, Crim Tartary's monarch.'

'Crim Tartary's usurper, gallant Hedzoff! Crim Tartary's grim tyrant, honest Hedzoff!' said the Prince, on the balcony, quite sarcastically.

'A soldier, Prince, must needs obey his orders: mine are to help his Majesty Padella. And also (though alack that I should say it!) to seize wherever I should light upon him –'

'First catch your hare! ha, Hedzoff!' exclaimed his Royal Highness.

'– On the body of *Giglio*, whilome Prince of Paflagonia,'

Hedzoff went on, with indescribable emotion. 'My Prince, give up your sword without ado. Look! we are thirty thousand men to one!'

'Give up my sword! Giglio give up his sword!' cried the Prince; and stepping well forward on to the balcony, the royal youth, *without preparation*, delivered a speech so magnificent, that no report can do justice to it. It was all in blank verse (in which, from this time, he invariably spoke, as more becoming his majestic station). It lasted for three days and three nights, during which not a single person who heard him was tired, or remarked the difference between daylight and dark. The soldiers only cheering tremendously, when occasionally, once in nine hours, the Prince paused to suck an orange, which Jones took out of the bag. He explained, in terms which we say we shall not attempt to convey, the whole history of the previous transaction, and his determination not only not to give up his sword, but to assume his rightful crown; and at the end of this extraordinary, this truly *gigantic* effort, Captain Hedzoff flung up his helmet, and cried, 'Hurray! Hurray! Long live King Giglio!'

Such were the consequences of having employed his time well at College!

When the excitement had ceased, beer was ordered out for the army, and their Sovereign himself did not disdain a little! And now it was with some alarm that Captain Hedzoff told him his division was only the advanced guard of the Paflagonian contingent, hastening to King Padella's aid. The main force being a day's march in the rear under his Royal Highness Prince Bulbo.

'We will wait here, good friend, to beat the Prince,' his Majesty said, 'and *then* will make his royal Father wince.'

15

We return to Rosalba

KING PADELLA made very similar proposals to Rosalba to those which she had received from the various Princes who, as we have seen, had fallen in love with her. His Majesty was a widower, and offered to marry his fair captive that instant, but she declined his invitation in her usual polite gentle manner, stating that Prince Giglio was her love, and that any other union was out of the question. Having tried tears and supplications in vain, this violent-tempered monarch menaced her with threats and tortures; but she declared she would rather suffer all these than accept the hand of her father's murderer, who left her finally, uttering the most awful imprecations, and bidding her prepare for death on the following morning.

All night long the King spent in advising how he should get rid of this obdurate young creature. Cutting off her head was much too easy a death for her; hanging was so common in his Majesty's dominions that it no longer afforded him any sport: finally, he bethought himself of a pair of fierce lions which had lately been sent to him as presents, and he determined, with these ferocious brutes, to hunt poor Rosalba down. Adjoining his castle was an amphitheatre where the Prince indulged in bull-baiting, rat-hunting, and other ferocious sports. The two lions were kept in a cage under this place; their roaring might be heard over the whole city, the inhabitants of which, I am sorry to say, thronged in numbers to see a poor young lady gobbled up by two wild beasts.

The King took his place in the royal box, having the officers of the Court around and the Count Hogginarmo by his side, upon whom his Majesty was observed to look very fiercely; the fact is, royal spies had told the monarch of Hogginarmo's behaviour, his proposals to Rosalba, and his offer to fight for the crown. Black as thunder looked King Padella at this proud noble, as they sat in the front seats of the theatre waiting to see the tragedy whereof poor Rosalba was to be the heroine.

At length that Princess was brought out in her night-gown, with all her beautiful hair falling down her back, and looking so pretty that even the beefeaters and keepers of the wild animals wept plentifully at seeing her. And she walked with her poor little feet (only luckily the arena was covered with sawdust), and went and leaned up against a great stone in the centre of the amphitheatre, round which the Court and the people were seated in boxes with bars before them, for fear of the great, fierce, red-maned, black-throated, long-tailed, roaring, bellowing, rushing lions. And now the gates

were opened, and with a wurrawarrurawarar two great lean, hungry, roaring lions rushed out of their den, where they had been kept for three weeks on nothing but a little toast-and-water, and dashed straight up to the stone where poor Rosalba was waiting. Commend her to your patron saints, all you kind people, for she is in a dreadful state.

There was a hum and a buzz all through the circus, and the fierce King Padella even felt a little compassion. But Count

Hogginarmo, seated by his Majesty, roared out, 'Hurray! Now for it! Soo-soo-soo!' that nobleman being uncommonly angry still at Rosalba's refusal of him.

But O strange event! O remarkable circumstance! O extraordinary coincidence, which I am sure none of you could *by any possibility* have divined! When the lions came to Rosalba, instead of devouring her with their great teeth, it was with kisses they gobbled her up! They licked her pretty feet, they nuzzled their noses in her lap, they moo'd, they seemed to say, 'Dear, dear sister, don't you recollect your brothers in the forest?' And she put her pretty white arms round their tawny necks, and kissed them.

King Padella was immensely astonished. The Count Hogginarmo was extremely disgusted. 'Pooh!' the Count cried. 'Gammon!' exclaimed his Lordship. 'These lions are tame beasts come from Wombwell's or Astley's. It is a shame to put people off in this way. I believe they are little boys dressed up in door-mats. They are no lions at all.'

'Ha!' said the King, 'you dare to say "gammon" to your Sovereign, do you? These lions are no lions at all, aren't they? Ho! my beefeaters! Ho! my body-guard! Take this Count Hogginarmo and fling him into the circus! Give him a sword and buckler, let him keep his armour on, and his weather-eye out, and fight these lions.'

The haughty Hogginarmo laid down his opera-glass, and looked scowling round at the King and his attendants. 'Touch me not, dogs!' he said, 'or by St. Nicholas the Elder, I will gore you! Your Majesty thinks Hogginarmo is afraid? No, not of a hundred thousand lions! Follow me down into the circus, King Padella, and match thyself against one of yon brutes. Thou darest not. Let them both come on, then!' And opening a grating of the box, he jumped lightly down into the circus.

Wurra wurra wurra wur-aw-aw-aw!!!
In about two minutes
The Count Hogginarmo was
GOBBLED UP
by
those lions,
bones, boots, and all,
and
There was an
End of him.

At this, the King said, 'Serve him right, the rebellious ruffian! And now, as those lions won't eat that young woman –'

'Let her off! – let her off!' cried the crowd.

'NO!' roared the King. 'Let the beefeaters go down and chop her into small pieces. If the lions defend her, let the archers shoot them to death. That hussy shall die in tortures!'

'A-a-ah!' cried the crowd. 'Shame! shame!'

'Who dares cry out shame?' cried the furious potentate (so little can tyrants command their passions). 'Fling any scoundrel who says a word down among the lions!' I warrant you there was a dead silence then, which was broken by a Pang arang pang pangkarangpang; and a Knight and a Herald rode in at the farther end of the circus. The Knight, in full armour, with his vizor up, and bearing a letter on the point of his lance.

'Ha!' exclaimed the King, 'by my fay, 'tis Elephant and Castle, pursuivant of my brother of Paflagonia; and the Knight, an my memory serves me, is the gallant Captain Hedzoff! What news from Paflagonia, gallant Hedzoff? Elephant and Castle, beshrew me, thy trumpeting must have made thee thirsty. What will my trusty herald like to drink?'

'Bespeaking first safe conduct from your Lordship,' said Captain Hedzoff, 'before we take a drink of anything, permit us to deliver our King's message.'

113

'My Lordship, Ha!' said Crim Tartary, frowning terrifically. 'That title soundeth strange in the anointed ears of a crowned King. Straightway speak out your message, Knight and Herald!'

Reining up his charger in a most elegant manner close under the King's balcony, Hedzoff turned to the herald, and bade him begin.

Elephant and Castle, dropping his trumpet over his shoulder, took a large sheet of paper out of his hat, and began to read:

'O Yes! O Yes! O Yes! Know all men by these presents, that we, Giglio, King of Paflagonia, Grand Duke of Cappadocia, Sovereign Prince of Turkey and the Sausage Islands, having assumed our rightful throne and title, long time falsely borne by our usurping Uncle, styling himself King of Paflagonia –'

'Ha!' growled Padella.

'Hereby summon the false traitor, Padella, calling himself King of Crim Tartary' –

The King's curses were dreadful. 'Go on, Elephant and Castle!' said the intrepid Hedzoff.

'– To release from cowardly imprisonment his liege lady and rightful Sovereign, ROSALBA, Queen of Crim Tartary, and restore her to her royal throne: in default of which, I, Giglio, proclaim the said Padella sneak, traitor, humbug, usurper, and coward. I challenge him to meet me, with fists or with pistols, with battle-axe or sword, with blunderbuss or singlestick, alone or at the head of his army, on foot or on horseback; and will prove my words upon his wicked ugly body!'

'God save the King!' said Captain Hedzoff, executing a demivolte, two semilunes, and three caracols.

'Is that all?' said Padella, with the terrific calm of concentrated fury.

'That, sir, is all my royal master's message. Here is his Majesty's letter in autograph, and here is his glove, and if any gentleman of Crim Tartary chooses to find fault with his Majesty's expressions, I, Tuffskin Hedzoff, Captain of the Guard, am very much at his service,' and he waved his lance, and looked at the assembly all round.

'And what says my good brother of Paflagonia, my dear son's father-in-law, to this rubbish?' asked the King.

'The King's uncle hath been deprived of the crown he unjustly wore,' said Hedzoff gravely. 'He and his ex-minister, Glumboso, are now in prison waiting the sentence of my royal master. After the battle of Bombardaro –'

'Of what?' asked the surprised Padella.

'Of Bombardaro, where my liege, his present Majesty, would have performed prodigies of valour, but that the whole of his uncle's army came over to our side, with the exception of Prince Bulbo.'

'Ah! my boy, my boy, my Bulbo was no traitor!' cried Padella.

'Prince Bulbo, far from coming over to us, ran away, sir; but I caught him. The Prince is a prisoner in our army, and the most terrific tortures await him if a hair of the Princess Rosalba's head is injured.'

'Do they?' exclaimed the furious Padella, who was now perfectly *livid* with rage. 'Do they indeed? So much the worse for Bulbo. I've twenty sons as lovely each as Bulbo. Not one but is as fit to reign as Bulbo. Whip, whack, flog, starve, rack, punish, torture Bulbo – break all his bones – roast him or flay him alive – pull all his pretty teeth out one by one! But justly dear as Bulbo is to me – Joy of my eyes, fond treasure of my soul! – Ha, ha, ha, ha! revenge is dearer still. Ho! torturers, rack-men, executioners – light up the fires and make the pincers hot! get lots of boiling lead! – Bring out ROSALBA!'

16

How Hedzoff rode back again to King Giglio

CAPTAIN HEDZOFF rode away when King Padella uttered this cruel command, having done his duty in delivering the message with which his royal master had entrusted him. Of course he was very sorry for Rosalba, but what could he do?

So he returned to King Giglio's camp, and found the young monarch in a disturbed state of mind, smoking cigars in the royal tent. His Majesty's agitation was not appeased by the news that was brought by his ambassador. 'The brutal ruthless ruffian royal wretch!' Giglio exclaimed. 'As England's poesy has well remarked, "The man that lays his hand upon a woman, save in the way of kindness, is a villain." Ha, Hedzoff?'

'That he is, your Majesty,' said the attendant.

'And didst thou see her flung into the oil? and didn't the soothing oil – the emollient oil, refuse to boil, good Hedzoff – and to spoil the fairest lady ever eyes did look on?'

'Faith, good my liege, I had no heart to look and see a beauteous lady boiling down; I took your royal message to Padella, and bore his back to you. I told him you would hold Prince Bulbo answerable. He only said that he had twenty sons as good as Bulbo, and forthwith he bade the ruthless executioners proceed.'

'O cruel father – O unhappy son,' cried the King. 'Go, some of you, and bring Prince Bulbo hither.'

Bulbo was brought in chains, looking very uncomfortable. Though a prisoner, he had been tolerably happy, perhaps

Poor Bulbo is ordered for execution

because his mind was at rest, and all the fighting was over, and he was playing at marbles with his guards, when the King sent for him.

'O, my poor Bulbo,' said his Majesty, with looks of infinite compassion, 'hast thou heard the news (for you see Giglio wanted to break the thing gently to the Prince), thy brutal father has condemned Rosalba – p-p-p-ut her to death, P-p-p-prince Bulbo!'

'What, killed Betsinda, Boo-hoo-hoo,' cried out Bulbo. 'Betsinda! pretty Betsinda! dear Betsinda! She was the dearest little girl in the world. I love her better twenty thousand times even than Angelica,' and he went on expressing his grief in so hearty and unaffected a manner, that the King was quite touched by it, and said, shaking Bulbo's hand, that he wished he had known Bulbo sooner.

Bulbo, quite unconsciously, and meaning for the best, offered to come and sit with his Majesty, and smoke a cigar with him, and console him. The *royal kindness* supplied Bulbo with a cigar; he had not had one, he said, since he was taken prisoner.

And now think what must have been the feelings of the most *merciful of monarchs*, when he informed his prisoner that, in consequence of King Padella's *cruel and dastardly behaviour* to Rosalba, Prince Bulbo must instantly be executed! The noble Giglio could not restrain his tears, nor could the Grenadiers, nor the officers, nor could Bulbo himself, when the matter was explained to him, and he was brought to understand that his Majesty's promise, of course, was *above every* thing, and Bulbo must submit. So poor Bulbo was led out. Hedzoff trying to console him, by pointing out that if he had won the battle of Bombardaro, he might have hanged Prince Giglio. 'Yes! But that is no comfort to me now!' said poor Bulbo; nor indeed was it, poor fellow.

He was told the business would be done the next morning at eight, and was taken back to his dungeon, where every attention was paid to him. The gaoler's wife sent him tea, and the turnkey's daughter begged him to write his name in her album, where a many gentlemen had wrote it on like occasions! 'Bother your album!' says Bulbo. The Undertaker came and measured him for the handsomest coffin which

money could buy – even this didn't console Bulbo. The Cook brought him dishes which he once used to like; but he wouldn't touch them: he sat down and began writing an adieu to Angelica, as the clock kept always ticking, and the hands drawing nearer to next morning. The Barber came in at night, and offered to shave him for the next day. Prince Bulbo kicked him away, and went on writing a few words to Princess Angelica, as the clock kept always ticking, and the hands hopping nearer and nearer to next morning. He got up on the top of a hat-box, on the top of a chair, on the top of his bed, on the top of his table, and looked out to see whether he might escape as the clock kept always ticking and the hands drawing nearer, and nearer, and nearer.

But looking out of the window was one thing, and jumping another: and the town clock struck seven. So he got into bed for a little sleep, but the gaoler came and woke him, and said, 'Git up, your Royal Ighness, if you please, it's *ten minutes to eight.*'

So poor Bulbo got up: he had gone to bed in his clothes (the lazy boy), and he shook himself, and said he didn't mind

121

about dressing, or having any breakfast, thank you; and he saw the soldiers who had come for him. 'Lead on!' he said; and they led the way, deeply affected; and they came into the courtyard, and out into the square, and there was King Giglio come to take leave of him, and his Majesty most kindly shook hands with him, and the *gloomy procession* marched on: when hark!

Haw – wurraw – wurraw – aworr!

A roar of wild beasts was heard. And who should come riding into the town, frightening away the boys, and even the beadle and policeman, but ROSALBA!

The fact is, that when Captain Hedzoff entered into the court of Snapdragon Castle, and was discoursing with King Padella, the Lions made a dash at the open gate, gobbled up the six beefeaters in a jiffy, and away they went with Rosalba on the back of one of them, and they carried her,

turn and turn about, till they came to the city where Prince
Giglio's army was encamped.

When the KING heard of the QUEEN'S arrival, you may
think how he rushed out of his breakfast-room to hand her
Majesty off her Lion! The Lions were grown as fat as Pigs
now, having had Hogginarmo and all those beefeaters, and
were so tame, anybody might pat them.

While Giglio knelt (most gracefully) and helped the
Princess, Bulbo, for his part, rushed up and kissed the Lion.
He flung his arms round the forest monarch; he hugged him,

and laughed and cried for joy. 'O you darling old beast, O, how glad I am to see you, and the dear, dear Bets – that is, Rosalba.'

'What, is it you? poor Bulbo,' said the Queen. 'O, how glad I am to see you'; and she gave him her hand to kiss. King Giglio slapped him most kindly on the back, and said, 'Bulbo, my boy, I am delighted, for your sake, that her Majesty has arrived.'

'So am I,' said Bulbo; 'and *you know why*.' Captain Hedzoff here came up. 'Sire, it is half past eight: shall we proceed with the execution?'

'Execution, what for?' asked Bulbo.

'An officer only knows his orders,' replied Captain Hedzoff, showing his warrant, on which his Majesty King Giglio smilingly said, 'Prince Bulbo was reprieved this time,' and most graciously invited him to breakfast.

17

How a tremendous battle took place,
and who won it

As soon as King Padella heard, what we know already, that his victim, the lovely Rosalba, had escaped him, his Majesty's fury knew no bounds, and he pitched the Lord Chancellor, Lord Chamberlain, and every officer of the crown whom he could set eyes on, into the cauldron of boiling oil prepared for the Princess. Then he ordered out his whole army, horse, foot, and artillery; and set forth at the head of an innumerable host, and I should think twenty thousand drummers, trumpeters, and fifers.

King Giglio's advanced guard, you may be sure, kept that monarch acquainted with the enemy's dealings, and he was in no wise disconcerted. He was much too polite to alarm the Princess, his lovely guest, with any unnecessary rumours of battles impending; on the contrary, he did everything to amuse and divert her; gave her a most elegant breakfast, dinner, lunch, and got up a ball for her that evening, when he danced with her every single dance.

Poor Bulbo was taken into favour again, and allowed to go quite free now. He had new clothes given him, was called 'My good cousin' by his Majesty, and was treated with the greatest distinction by everybody. But it was easy to see he was very melancholy. The fact is, the sight of Betsinda, who looked perfectly lovely in an elegant new dress, set poor Bulbo frantic in love with her again. And he never thought about Angelica, now Princess Bulbo, whom he had left at home, and who, as we know, did not care much about him.

The King, dancing the twenty-fifth polka with Rosalba, remarked with wonder the ring she wore; and then Rosalba told him how she had got it from Gruffanuff, who no doubt had picked it up when Angelica flung it away.

'Yes,' says the Fairy Blackstick, who had come to see the young people, and who had very likely certain plans regarding them. 'That ring I gave the Queen, Giglio's mother, who was not, saving your presence, a very wise woman; it is enchanted, and whoever wears it looks beautiful in the eyes of the world. I made poor Prince Bulbo, when he was christened, the present of a rose which made him look handsome while he had it; but he gave it to Angelica, who instantly looked beautiful again, whilst Bulbo relapsed into his natural plainness.'

'Rosalba needs no ring, I am sure,' says Giglio, with a low bow. 'She is beautiful enough, in my eyes, without any enchanted aid.'

'O, sir!' said Rosalba.

'Take off the ring and try,' said the King, and resolutely drew the ring off her finger. In *his* eyes she looked just as handsome as before.

The King was thinking of throwing the ring away, as it was so dangerous and made all the people so mad about Rosalba; but being a Prince of great humour, and good-humour too, he cast eyes upon a poor youth who happened to be looking on very disconsolately, and said –

'Bulbo, my poor lad! come and try on this ring. The Princess Rosalba makes it a present to you.' The magic properties of this ring were uncommonly strong, for no sooner had Bulbo put it on, but lo and behold, he appeared a personable, agreeable young Prince enough – with a fine complexion, fair hair, rather stout, and with bandy legs; but these were encased in such a beautiful pair of yellow morocco boots that nobody remarked them. And Bulbo's spirits rose up almost immediately after he had looked in the glass, and he talked to their Majesties in the most lively, agreeable manner, and danced opposite the Queen with one of the prettiest maids of honour, and after looking at her Majesty, could not help saying – 'How very odd; she is very pretty, but not so *extraordinarily* handsome.' 'Oh no, by no means!' says the Maid of Honour.

'But what care I, dear sir,' says the Queen, who overheard them, 'if *you* think I am good-looking enough?'

His Majesty's glance in reply to this affectionate speech was such that no painter could draw it. And the Fairy Blackstick said, 'Bless you, my darling children! Now you are united and happy; and now you see what I said from the first, that a little misfortune has done you both good. *You*, Giglio, had you been bred in prosperity, would scarcely have learned to read or write – you would have been idle and extravagant, and could not have been a good King as you now will be. You, Rosalba, would have been so flattered, that your little head might have been turned like Angelica's, who thought herself too good for Giglio.'

'As if anybody could be good enough for *him*,' cried Rosalba.

'Oh, you, you darling!' says Giglio. And so she was; and he was just holding out his arms in order to give her a hug before the whole company, when a messenger came rushing in, and said, 'My Lord, the enemy!'

'To arms!' cries Giglio.

'Oh, Mercy!' says Rosalba, and fainted of course. He snatched one kiss from her lips, and rushed *forth to the field* of battle!

The Fairy had provided King Giglio with a suit of armour, which was not only embroidered all over with jewels, and blinding to your eyes to look at, but was water-proof, gun-proof, and sword-proof; so that in the midst of the very hottest battles his Majesty rode about as calmly as if he had been a British Grenadier at Alma. Were I engaged in fighting for my country, *I* should like such a suit of armour as Prince Giglio wore; but, you know, he was a Prince of a fairy tale, and they always have these wonderful things.

Besides the fairy armour, the Prince had a fairy horse, which would gallop at any pace you please; and a fairy sword, which would lengthen, and run through a whole regiment of enemies at once. With such a weapon at command, I wonder, for my part, he thought of ordering his army out; but forth they all came, in magnificent new uniforms; Hedzoff and the Prince's two college friends each commanding a division, and his Majesty prancing in person at the head of them all.

Ah! if I had the pen of a Sir Archibald Alison, my dear friends, would I not now entertain you with the account of a most tremendous shindy? Should not fine blows be struck? dreadful wounds be delivered? arrows darken the air? cannon balls crash through the battalions? cavalry charge infantry? infantry pitch into cavalry? bugles blow; drums beat; horses neigh; fifes sing; soldiers roar, swear, hurray; officers shout out, 'Forward, my men!' 'This way, lads!' 'Give it 'em, boys.' 'Fight for King Giglio, and the cause of right!' 'King Padella for ever!' Would I not describe all this, I say, and in the very finest language, too? But this humble pen does not possess the skill necessary for the description of combats. In a word, the overthrow of King Padella's army was so complete, that if they had been Russians you could not have wished them to be more utterly smashed and confounded.

As for that usurping monarch, having performed acts of valour much more considerable than could be expected of a royal ruffian and usurper, who had such a bad cause, and who was so cruel to women – as for King Padella, I say, when his army ran away, the King ran away too, kicking his first general, Prince Punchikoff, from his saddle, and galloping away on the Prince's horse, having, indeed, had twenty-five or twenty-six of his own shot under him. Hedzoff coming up, and finding Punchikoff down, as you may imagine, very speedily disposed of *him*. Meanwhile King Padella was scampering off as hard as his horse could lay legs to ground. Fast as he scampered, I promise you somebody else galloped faster; and that individual, as no doubt you are aware, was the Royal Giglio, who kept bawling out, 'Stay, traitor! Turn, miscreant, and defend thyself! Stand, tyrant, coward, ruffian, royal wretch, till I cut thy ugly head from thy usurping shoulders!' And, with his fairy sword, which elongated itself at will, his Majesty kept poking and prodding Padella in the back, until that wicked monarch roared with anguish.

When he was fairly brought to bay, Padella turned and dealt Prince Giglio a prodigious crack over the sconce with his battle-axe, a most enormous weapon, which had cut down I don't know how many regiments in the course of the afternoon. But, Law bless you! though the blow fell right down on his Majesty's helmet, it made no more impression than if Padella had struck him with a pat of butter: his battle-axe crumpled up in Padella's hand, and the Royal Giglio laughed for very scorn at the impotent efforts of that atrocious usurper.

At the ill success of his blow the Crim Tartar monarch was justly irritated. 'If,' says he to Giglio, 'you ride a fairy horse, and wear fairy armour, what on earth is the use of my hitting you? I may as well give myself up a prisoner at once. Your Majesty won't, I suppose, be so mean as to strike a poor fellow who can't strike again?'

The justice of Padella's remark struck the magnanimous Giglio. 'Do you yield yourself a prisoner, Padella?' says he.

'Of course, I do,' says Padella.

'Do you acknowledge Rosalba as your rightful Queen, and give up the crown and all your treasures to your rightful mistress?'

'If I must I must,' says Padella, who was naturally very sulky.

By this time King Giglio's aides-de-camp had come up, whom his Majesty ordered to bind the prisoner. And they tied his hands behind him, and bound his legs tight under his horse, having set him with his face to the tail; and in this fashion he was led back to King Giglio's quarters, and thrust into the very dungeon where young Bulbo had been confined.

Padella (who was a very different person in the depth of his distress, to Padella, the proud wearer of the Crim Tartar crown), now most affectionately and earnestly asked to see his son – his dear eldest boy – his darling Bulbo; and that good-natured young man never once reproached his haughty parent for his unkind conduct the day before, when he would have left Bulbo to be shot without any pity, but came to see his father, and spoke to him through the grating of the door, beyond which he was not allowed to go; and brought him some sandwiches from the grand supper which his Majesty was giving above stairs, in honour of the brilliant victory which had just been achieved.

'I cannot stay with you long, sir,' says Bulbo, who was in his best ball dress, as he handed his father in the prog, 'I am engaged to dance the next quadrille with her Majesty Queen Rosalba, and I hear the fiddles playing at this very moment.'

So Bulbo went back to the ball-room, and the wretched Padella ate his s olitary supper in silence and tears.

All was now joy in King Giglio's circle. Dancing, feasting, fun, illuminations, and jollifications of all sorts ensued. The people through whose villages they passed were ordered to illuminate their cottages at night, and scatter flowers on the roads during the day. They were requested, and I promise you they did not like to refuse, to serve the troops liberally with eatables and wine; besides, the army was enriched by the immense quantity of plunder which was found in King Padella's camp, and taken from his soldiers; who (after they had given up everything) were allowed to fraternize with the conquerors; and the united forces marched back by easy stages towards King Giglio's capital, his royal banner and that of Queen Rosalba being carried in front of the troops. Hedzoff was made a Duke and a Field Marshal. Smith and Jones were promoted to be Earls; the Crim Tartar Order of the Pumpkin and the Paflagonian decoration of the Cucumber were freely distributed by their Majesties to the army. Queen Rosalba wore the Paflagonian Ribbon of the Cucumber across her riding habit, whilst King Giglio never appeared without the grand Cordon of the Pumpkin. How the people cheered them as they rode along side by side! They were pronounced to be the handsomest couple ever seen: that was a matter of course; but they really *were* very handsome, and, had they been otherwise, would have looked so, they were so happy! Their Majesties were never separated during the whole day, but breakfasted, dined, and supped together always, and rode side by side, interchanging elegant compliments, and indulging in the most delightful conversation. At night, her Majesty's ladies of honour (who had all rallied round her the day after King Padella's defeat), came and conducted her to the apartments prepared for her; whilst King Giglio, surrounded by his gentlemen, withdrew to his own Royal quarters. It was agreed they should be married as soon as they reached the capital, and orders were dispatched to the Archbishop of Blombodinga, to hold himself in readiness to perform the interesting ceremony. Duke Hedzoff carried the message, and gave instructions to have the Royal Castle splendidly refurnished and painted afresh. The Duke seized Glumboso, the Ex-Prime Minister, and made him refund that considerable sum of money which the old scoundrel had secreted out of the late King's treasure. He also clapped Valoroso into prison (who, by the way, had been dethroned for some considerable period past), and when the Ex-Monarch weakly remonstrated, Hedzoff said, 'A soldier, Sir, knows but his duty; my orders are to lock you up along with the Ex-King Padella, whom I have brought hither a prisoner under guard.' So these two Ex-Royal personages were sent for a year to the House of Correction, and thereafter were obliged to become monks of the severest Order of Flagellants, in which state, by fasting, by vigils, by flogging (which they administered to one another, humbly but resolutely), no doubt they exhibited a repentance for their past misdeeds, usurpations, and private and public crimes.

As for Glumboso, that rogue was sent to the galleys, and never had an opportunity to steal any more.

18

How they all journeyed back to the capital

THE Fairy Blackstick, by whose means this young King
and Queen had certainly won their respective Crowns back,
would come not unfrequently, to pay them a little visit – as
they were riding in their triumphal progress towards Giglio's
capital – change her wand into a pony, and travel by their
Majesties' side, giving them the very best advice. I am not
sure that King Giglio did not think the Fairy and her advice
rather a bore, fancying it was his own valour and merits
which had put him on his throne, and conquered Padella:
and, in fine, I fear he rather gave himself airs towards his
best friend and patroness. She exhorted him to deal justly
by his subjects, to draw mildly on the taxes, never to break
his promise when he had once given it – and in all respects to
be a good King.

'A good King, my dear Fairy!' cries Rosalba. 'Of course
he will. Break his promise! can you fancy my Giglio would
ever do anything so improper, so unlike him? No! never!'
And she looked fondly towards Giglio, whom she thought a
pattern of perfection.

'Why is Fairy Blackstick always advising me, and telling
me how to manage my government, and warning me to keep
my word? Does she suppose that I am not a man of sense,
and a man of honour?' asks Giglio, testily. 'Methinks she
rather presumes upon her position.'

'Hush! dear Giglio,' says Rosalba. 'You know Blackstick has been very kind to us, and we must not offend her.'

But the Fairy was not listening to Giglio's testy observations, she had fallen back, and was trotting on her pony now, by Master Bulbo's side, who rode a donkey, and made himself generally beloved in the army by his cheerfulness, kindness, and good-humour to everybody. He was eager to see his darling Angelica. He thought there never was such a charming being. Blackstick did not tell him it was the possession of the Magic Rose that made Angelica so lovely in his eyes. She brought him the very best accounts of his little wife, whose misfortunes and humiliations had indeed very greatly improved her; and you see, she could whisk off on her wand a hundred miles in a minute, and be back in no time, and so carry polite messages from Bulbo to Angelica, and from Angelica to Bulbo, and comfort that young man upon his journey.

When the Royal party arrived at the last stage before you reach Blombodinga, who should be in waiting, in her carriage there with her lady of honour by her side, but the Princess Angelica. She rushed into her husband's arms, scarcely stopping to make a passing curtsey to the King and Queen. She had no eyes but for Bulbo, who appeared perfectly lovely to her on account of the fairy ring which he wore; whilst she herself, wearing the magic rose in her bonnet, seemed entirely beautiful to the enraptured Bulbo.

A splendid luncheon was served to the Royal party, of which the Archbishop, the Chancellor, the Duke Hedzoff, Countess Gruffanuff, and all our friends partook. The Fairy Blackstick being seated on the left of King Giglio, with Bulbo and Angelica beside. You could hear the joy-bells ringing in the capital, and the guns which the citizens were firing off in honour of their Majesties.

'What can have induced that hideous old Gruffanuff to dress herself up in such an absurd way? Did you ask her

to be your bridesmaid, my dear?' says Giglio to Rosalba.
'What a figure of fun Gruffy is!'

Gruffy was seated opposite their Majesties, between the
Archbishop and the Lord Chancellor, and a figure of fun she
certainly was, for she was dressed in a low white silk dress,
with lace over, a wreath of white roses on her wig, a splendid
lace veil, and her yellow old neck was covered with diamonds.
She ogled the King in such a manner, that his Majesty burst
out laughing.

'Eleven o'clock!' cries Giglio, as the great Cathedral bell
of Blombodinga tolled that hour. 'Gentlemen and ladies, we
must be starting. Archbishop, you must be at church I think
before twelve?'

'We must be at church before twelve,' sighs out Gruffanuff in a languishing voice, hiding her old face behind her
fan.

'And then I shall be the happiest man in my dominions,'
cries Giglio, with an elegant bow to the blushing Rosalba.

'O, my Giglio! O, my dear Majesty!' exclaims Gruffanuff; 'and can it be that this happy moment at length has
arrived —'

'Of course it has arrived,' says the King.

'— And that I am about to become the enraptured bride
of my adored Giglio!' continues Gruffanuff. 'Lend me a
smelling-bottle, somebody. I certainly shall faint with joy.'

'*You* my bride?' roars out Giglio.

'*You* marry my Prince?' cries poor little Rosalba.

'Pooh! Nonsense! The woman's mad!' exclaims the King.
And all the courtiers exhibited by their countenances and
expressions, marks of surprise, or ridicule, or incredulity, or
wonder.

'I should like to know who else is going to be married, if
I am not?' shrieks out Gruffanuff. 'I should like to know
if King Giglio is a gentleman, and if there is such a thing as

justice in Paflagonia? Lord Chancellor! my Lord Archbishop! will your Lordships sit by and see a poor, fond, con-
fiding, tender creature put upon? Has not Prince Giglio
promised to marry his Barbara? Is not this Giglio's signature? Does not this paper declare that he is mine, and only
mine?' And she handed to his Grace the Archbishop the
document which the Prince signed that evening, when she
wore the magic ring, and Giglio drank so much champagne.
And the old Archbishop, taking out his eye-glasses, read –
' "This is to give notice, that I, Giglio, only son of Savio,
King of Paflagonia, hereby promise to marry the charming
Barbara Griselda Countess Gruffanuff, and widow of the late
Jenkins Gruffanuff, Esq." '

'H'm,' says the Archbishop, 'the document is certainly
a – a document.'

'Phoo,' says the Lord Chancellor, 'the signature is not in
his Majesty's handwriting.' Indeed, since his studies at
Bosforo, Giglio had made an immense improvement in cali-
graphy.

'Is it your handwriting, Giglio?' cries the Fairy Blackstick, with an awful severity of countenance.

'Y – y – y – es,' poor Giglio gasps out, 'I had quite forgotten the confounded paper: she can't mean to hold me by
it. You old wretch, what will you take to let me off? Help
the Queen, someone – her Majesty has fainted.'

'Chop her head off!'⎫ exclaim the impetuous Hed-
'Smother the old witch!'⎬ zoff, the ardent Smith, and
'Pitch her into the river!'⎭ the faithful Jones.

But Gruffanuff flung her arms round the Archbishop's
neck, and bellowed out, 'Justice, justice, my Lord Chancellor!' so loudly, that her piercing shrieks caused everybody to pause. As for Rosalba, she was borne away lifeless
by her ladies; and you may imagine the look of agony which
Giglio cast towards that lovely being, as his hope, his joy,

his darling, his all in all, was thus removed, and in her place the horrid old Gruffanuff rushed up to his side, and once more shrieked out, 'Justice, justice!'

'Won't you take that sum of money which Glumboso hid?' says Giglio: 'two hundred and eighteen thousand millions, or thereabouts. It's a handsome sum.'

'I will have that and you too!' says Gruffanuff.

'Let us throw the crown jewels into the bargain,' gasps out Giglio.

'I will wear them by my Giglio's side!' says Gruffanuff.

'Will half, three-quarters, five-sixths, nineteen-twentieths, of my kingdom do, Countess?' asks the trembling monarch.

'What were all Europe to me without *you*, my Giglio?' cries Gruff, kissing his hand.

'I won't, I can't, I shan't – I'll resign the crown first,' shouts Giglio, tearing away his hand; but Gruff clung to it.

'I have a competency, my love,' she says, 'and with thee and a cottage thy Barbara will be happy.'

Giglio was half mad with rage by this time. 'I will not marry her,' says he. 'Oh, Fairy, Fairy, give me counsel!' And as he spoke he looked wildly round at the severe face of the Fairy Blackstick.

' "Why is Fairy Blackstick always advising me, and warning me to keep my word? Does she suppose that I am not a man of honour?" ' said the Fairy, quoting Giglio's own haughty words. He quailed under the brightness of her eyes; he felt that there was no escape for him from that awful Inquisition.

'Well, Archbishop,' said he, in a dreadful voice that made his Grace start, 'since this Fairy has led me to the height of happiness but to dash me down into the depths of despair, since I am to lose Rosalba, let me at least keep my honour. Get up, Countess, and let us be married; I can keep my word, but I can die afterwards.'

'O dear Giglio,' cries Gruffanuff, skipping up, 'I knew, I knew I could trust thee – I knew that my Prince was the soul of honour. Jump into your carriages, ladies and gentlemen, and let us go to church at once; and as for dying, dear Giglio, no, no: – thou wilt forget that insignificant little chambermaid of a queen – thou wilt live to be consoled by thy Barbara! She wishes to be a Queen, and not a Queen Dowager, my gracious Lord!' And hanging upon poor Giglio's arm, and leering and grinning in his face in the most disgusting manner, this old wretch tripped off in her white satin shoes, and jumped into the very carriage which had been got ready to convey Giglio and Rosalba to church. The cannons roared again, the bells peeled triple-bobmajors, the people came out flinging flowers upon the path of the royal bride and bridegroom, and Gruff looked out of the gilt coach window and bowed and grinned to them. Phoo! the horrid old wretch!

19

And now we come to the last scene in the pantomime

THE many ups and downs of her life had given the Princess Rosalba prodigious strength of mind, and that highly principled young woman presently recovered from her fainting-fit, out of which Fairy Blackstick, by a precious essence which the Fairy always carried in her pocket, awakened her. Instead of tearing her hair, crying, and bemoaning herself, and fainting again, as many young women would have done, Rosalba remembered that she owed an example of firmness to her subjects; and though she loved Giglio more than her life, was determined, as she told the Fairy, not to interfere between him and justice, or to cause him to break his royal word.

'I cannot marry him, but I shall love him always,' says she to Blackstick; 'I will go and be present at his marriage with the Countess, and sign the book, and wish them happy with all my heart. I will see, when I get home, whether I cannot make the new Queen some handsome presents. The Crim Tartary crown diamonds are uncommonly fine, and I shall never have any use for them. I will live and die unmarried like Queen Elizabeth, and, of course, I shall leave my crown to Giglio when I quit this world. Let us go and see them married, my dear Fairy, let me say one last farewell to him; and then, if you please, I will return to my own dominions.'

So the Fairy kissed Rosalba with peculiar tenderness, and

at once changed her wand into a very comfortable coach-and-four, with a steady coachman, and two respectable foot-men behind, and the Fairy and Rosalba got into the coach, which Angelica and Bulbo entered after them. As for honest Bulbo, he was blubbering in the most pathetic manner, quite overcome by Rosalba's misfortune. She was touched by the honest fellow's sympathy, promised to restore to him the confiscated estates of Duke Padella his father, and created him, as he sat there in the coach, Prince, Highness, and First Grandee of the Crim Tartar Empire. The coach moved on, and, being a fairy coach, soon came up with the bridal procession.

Before the ceremony at church it was the custom in Pafla-gonia, as it is in other countries, for the bride and bride-groom to sign the Contract of Marriage, which was to be wit-nessed by the Chancellor, Minister, Lord Mayor, and prin-cipal officers of state. Now, as the royal palace was being painted and furnished anew, it was not ready for the recep-tion of the King and his bride, who proposed at first to take up their residence at the Prince's palace, that one which Valoroso occupied when Angelica was born, and before he usurped the throne.

So the marriage party drove up to the palace: the digni-taries got out of their carriages and stood aside: poor Rosalba stepped out of her coach, supported by Bulbo, and stood al-most fainting up against the railings so as to have a last look of her dear Giglio. As for Blackstick, she, according to her custom, had flown out of the coach window in some inscrutable manner, and was now standing at the palace door.

Giglio came up the steps with his horrible bride on his arm, looking as pale as if he was going to execution. He only frowned at the Fairy Blackstick – he was angry with her, and thought she came to insult his misery.

'Get out of the way, pray,' says Gruffanuff, haughtily.
'I wonder why you are always poking your nose into other
people's affairs?'

'Are you determined to make this poor young man unhappy?' says Blackstick.

'To marry him, yes! What business is it of yours? Pray,
madam, don't say "you" to a Queen,' cries Gruffanuff.

'You won't take the money he offered you?'

'No.'

'You won't let him off his bargain, though you know you
cheated him when you made him sign the paper?'

'Impudence! Policemen, remove this woman!' cries Gruffanuff. And the policemen were rushing forward, but with a
wave of her wand the Fairy struck them all like so many
statues in their places.

'You won't take anything in exchange for your bond, Mrs Gruffanuff,' cries the Fairy, with awful severity. 'I speak for the last time.'

'No!' shrieks Gruffanuff, stamping with her foot. 'I'll have my husband, my husband, my husband!'

'YOU SHALL HAVE YOUR HUSBAND!' the Fairy Blackstick cried; and advancing a step, laid her hand upon the nose of the KNOCKER.

As she touched it, the brass nose seemed to elongate, the open mouth opened still wider, and uttered a roar which made everybody start. The eyes rolled wildly; the arms and legs uncurled themselves, writhed about, and seemed to lengthen with each twist; the knocker expanded into a figure in yellow livery, six feet high; the screws by which it was fixed to the door unloosed themselves, and JENKINS GRUFFANUFF once more trod the threshold off which he had been lifted more than twenty years ago!

'Master's not at home,' says Jenkins, just in his old voice; and Mrs Jenkins, giving a dreadful *youp*, fell down in a fit, in which nobody minded her.

For everybody was shouting, 'Huzzay! huzzay!' 'Hip, hip, hurray!' 'Long live the King and Queen!' 'Were such things ever seen?' 'No never, never, never!' 'The Fairy Blackstick for ever!'

The bells were ringing double peals, the guns roaring and banging most prodigiously. Bulbo was embracing everybody; the Lord Chancellor was flinging up his wig and shouting like a madman; Hedzoff had got the Archbishop round the waist, and they were dancing a jig for joy; and as for Giglio, I leave you to imagine what *he* was doing, and if he kissed Rosalba once, twice – twenty thousand times, I'm sure I don't think he was wrong.

So Gruffanuff opened the hall door with a low bow, just as

he had been accustomed to do, and they all went in and signed the book, and then they went to church and were married, and the Fairy Blackstick sailed away on her cane, and was never more heard of in Paflagonia.

AND HERE
ENDS THE FIRESIDE
PANTOMIME